TOEFL
托福文法與構句

李英松／著

前冊

esn't have a carefully developed plot. (主格補語) Whatever you decide will be f
that red bicycle. (介詞的受詞) Do you know what ha ed
詞) The p r gave whatever spots to the rest of my tune fi ndw
had other coat of enamel. (間接受詞) Roth mowed the ou
ve ho d out the weeds, while we weede ds.
ld n he roses. Give some consideration o se never
結, hours in the hot sun had 形容詞子句 當做形容
us feel as though the day would never end.
sist of of people and some that contain is a group
lang e language that we use during our childhoo
atio y 立子句（或稱主要子句），可以單獨存在成為
ge. 可以和另外一個獨立子句連結，The gymnasts and th
r d me 能完整表達意思。 William read The Washington Post
y s ion. (句 Our class is writing stories for the second graders at Thomson Elementary S
e to subway station, and I arrived at school on time. (兩個

自序

　　很多人在問，我們為什麼要學習英文文法，在回答這個問題之前，請讀者先大聲的朗誦下列七則一對母子在閒聊時的問與答：

問：兒子，最近不管在美國還是在台灣的政客，對於自己不利的訊息，一律稱之為假消息，對於自己有利的則叫做真消息。你的看法是如何？

答：媽，社會上充斥著太多錯誤的假訊息，讓人眼花撩亂。這些政客幾乎不認為自己有錯，只是怪別人亂放假消息。

問：兒子，當今台灣大賣場陸陸續續發現大量的過期食品，你看怎麼辦？

答：媽，很簡單，我認為立刻馬上去做下架的動作，並趕快的立即的去實行銷毀的動作。

問：兒子，你和女朋友交往有一段時間了，進展到什麼程度了？

答：媽，我的女朋友她非常孝順並且很節儉，我非常珍惜這段感情，因此現在目前是拉拉手，還沒到擁抱的動作，更沒達到接吻的動作。

問：兒子，今天那麼早起來，上班為什麼還遲到呢？

答：媽，我一早起床就上廁所，然後刷牙洗臉，然後運動，然後吃早餐，然後換衣服，然後坐捷運，然後打卡遲到，妳知道嗎？

問：兒子，我們上個星期天去麵館吃的牛肉麵，你喜歡嗎？

答：媽，妳講說所謂牛肉麵，一般來說，一方面看的感覺，另外一方面吃的感覺，對我而言，所謂喜歡不喜歡，是有太辣的感覺。

問：兒子，今天的天氣怎樣？

答：　媽，所謂今天的天氣，依據電視台的氣象報告，所謂溫度非常偏低，也有可能所謂的下雨，不過放心，我開車會非常小心謹慎，同時我會分享網友，對不對？

問：　兒子，和你同名同姓的同學，我好久沒有看到他了，他的功課好嗎？

答：　媽，我的同學他最近心情不太好，聽他說，前一陣子他和他的女朋友吵架之後情緒非常低落，妳知道嗎？當然會影響這次的期中考，他告訴我英文這科被當掉了，妳知道嗎？我把這壞消息分享給媽和爸。

　　請問讀者唸完上述七則對話之後，發現了什麼？有哪些不對勁？如果仍然未發現問題，請再大聲唸一遍，必定體會出對話之瑕疵所在。

　　筆者在此可以透漏，這對母子的對話，媽媽的問話，不管在用字遣詞，或者說話的流暢度，一點都沒問題。反觀兒子的答話卻充滿著奇奇怪怪的用語，諸如詞類混淆不清，主詞動詞誤用，雙重否定，畫蛇添足，用詞重複，造成邏輯不通，不知所云。

　　旅居美國三十餘年的筆者，每天打開電視觀看台灣的政論節目，新聞報導或歌唱談話節目，各個階層，每個角落，隨時可聽到如同這位兒子的說話方式。怎不令人憂心，好像細菌般傳染，一傳十，十傳百，人人習以為常相互模仿。

　　從小到大到老，我們所使用的本國語文，竟會產生語病，而英語文不是我們的母語，學習英文文法就顯得格外重要。

　　筆者始終認為英文文法，如同我們所修的數學、化學和物理學等的定理、定律或者方程式。這些原理，原則透過數學家、化學家、物理學家和語文學家經過數百年，甚至數千年不斷的演練，實驗和推敲而產生。生為後代子孫的我們，得賴以遵循，真的應驗了古人所言「前人種樹，後人乘涼」的名言。

　　本書有下列三個特點：

　　第一，以條列的方式，將英文文法規則一條一條的列出來，化繁為簡，讓讀者可以一目了然。

第二，完全以中文說明，並舉實例加以印證，引導讀者可以觸類旁通，消除對英文文法規則的恐懼。

第三，練習題以專章介紹，讀者可以自訂目標，以每日十題至二十題自我訓練，務必要達到完全了解 5WIH（What, Where, Which, Who, Whom & How）為止。

本書姊妹著作《托福字彙》上、中、下冊一、下冊二四冊，讀者如有機會配合研讀，當能相得益彰。依據托福測驗中心的統計，托福文法的考試，是我們台灣應考者的強項。針對如何加強讀者這方面的實力，是作者編著一系列有關托福考試書籍的動機，而讀者的鼓勵與支持，則是作者繼續收集資料編著書籍的原動力。

最後值得一提的事，在如何出版一本書的過程中，姪女李昭儀，姪子李鍊賦學會了一整套，諸如排版、設計、校對、印刷和發行。而筆者也見識到科技的進步，從數十年前打字機時代，如今是電腦大眾化的時代。古人說道「活到老，學到老」又有人說「老幹新枝」處處顯示老、中、青三代通力合作，才能使社會更進步。

目錄

第一章 ｜ 冠詞（Articles）

1. 雖然冠詞只有 a，an 和 the 三個字，但使用起來，卻相當複雜。

2. a 和 an 為不定冠詞，而 the 則為定冠詞。

3. 只要單數的普通名詞，不管是任何人、事、時、地、物，其第一個字母的發音為子音時用 a。但是第一個字母的發音為母音時則用 an。（a，e，i，o 和 u 為母首，其它的則為子音。要注意的是發音而非以字母為準。

   子音如 a man, a table, a chair, a piece of paper, a good teacher, a nice day, etc.

   母音如 an hour ago, an old lady, an egg, an ugly cat, etc.

4. 如果我們所談論的人、事、時、地、物等等為特定的，這就必須使用 the。

   如 the man in the room, the dog on the street, the book on the desk, the weather is good today, etc.

   有時候使用在複數且特定的名詞上，如 the workers of this company

5. 有些人認為 a 和 an 也是形容詞，因為 an orange 和 one orange 以及 an egg 和 one egg 等等沒有兩樣之故。

6. 從一般的普通名詞，變成特定的普通名詞時，要從 a 和 an 改用 the

   如 a book-----the book on my desk, an egg-----the egg in the bowl

7. 表示自然界或方向的普通名詞要用 the。如 the earth, the moon, the east, the west 之類。

8. 通常物質名詞或者專有名詞不加冠詞，但也有例外，如 the wind was very strong last night, the Republic of China, the United States of America

9. 專有名詞當形容詞時也要加 the，如 the Chinese story, the English book

10. 食品名詞不加冠詞，如 rice, wine, fish, ham

11. 抽象名詞和集合名詞不加冠詞，如 happiness, sadness, furniture, money

12. 形容詞的最高級要加 the，如 the biggest, the highest, the tallest

13. 形容詞加 the 就變成複數名詞，如 the handless=handless people, the poor=poor people

14. a 的成語有不一樣的意義，如 a lot of, a number of, give me a hand

15. the 的成語也是很多，如 by the pound, on the other hand, in the dark

16. 單數普通名詞加冠詞 a，an 或 the 時，與複數普通名詞的意義相同，如 A cat is a timid animal.=Cats are timid animal.=The cat is a timid animal.

17. 不定冠詞──指一般而言。

    a. He is a friend of mine.

    b. There is an elephant picture on the wall.

    c. It takes me an hour from my home to school.

18. 限定冠詞──指特定而言。

    a. The cat is black, and the dogs are white in his backyard.

    b. She loaned her picture to the museum.

19. 不可使用冠詞 a 或 an 在 kind of, type of, or sort of 之後。

    a. What kind of a sports car is this? (wrong)

       What kind of sports car is this? (right)

    b. I prefer this type of a shirt. (wrong)

       I prefer this type of shirt. (right)

    c. We went to the hardware store for a special sort of a wrench. (wrong)

       We went to the hardware store for a special sort of wrench. (right)

20. 當我們使用 a 或 an 在英文字母中時，必須遵守如下規則：

    A.　This is a B, C, D, G, J, K, P, Q, T, U, V, W, Y, Z.

    B.　This is an A, E, F, H, I, L, M, N, O, R, S, X.

      a. a fire but an F

      b. a sound but an S

c. a man but an M

d. a house but an H

21. 我們要知道 a/an 和 one，one and a/an 通常上是不能互換使用的，我們要使用 one 是當我們在計算時。如：

a. It was <u>one</u> coke we ordered, not two. (right)

It was <u>a</u> coke we ordered, not two. (wrong)

b. A knife is no good.　You need a screwdriver to do the job properly. (right)

One knife is no good.　You need one screwdriver to do the job properly. (wrong)

22. 基本上，下列情況的名詞不需使用冠詞。

A. 複數可數名詞：oranges, tomatoes

B. 不可數名詞：air, water

C. 專有名詞：William, John

D. 三餐：breakfast, lunch, tea, dinner, supper

a. Dinner is served.

b. William's at lunch.

c. Let's have breakfast.

d. We have tea at half past four.

e. At what time is supper?

E. 交通：by air, by sea, on foot, by bicycle, by boat, by bus, by train.

a. It saves a great deal of time to travel by air.

b. He traveled Europe by sea.

c. My children go to school on foot.

d. He came to school by bicycle.

e. Let us go by boat.

f. We traveled all over Maryland by bus.

g. My wife went to New York by train last week.

F. 顏色：red, yellow, blue, black, white, green

23. 在一個句子中，如果敘述的主詞是同一個，用一個冠詞；敘述的主詞不是同一個，則需要兩個以上的冠詞。如：

    a. The player and singer was in Taiwan last year.

       (player 和 singer 是指同一個人)

    b. A red and a blue shirt are in my closet.

       (red shirt 和 blue shirt 是指不同一件衣服)

24. 廣義來說，冠詞也是一種形容詞，因為有了它們，才能知悉名詞的數量，範圍等等。

    a. My brother, he changes jobs at least twice a year.

    b. The tall figure walking hurriedly through the park.

    c. An apple and an orange add substance to your diet.

    d. The children take a bus after-school activities.

    e. The winning artists display their works in the Town Hall.

    f. He lost his composure during the worse battle of the war.

    g. An argument raged between the two teams.

    h. A contestant with a soprano voice won the talent competition.

    i. A brief summary of World War I is in the first chapter.

    j. I like to walk in the rain, to sing in the shower, and to stamp in puddles.

第二章 | 副詞 (Adverbs)

1. 副詞是修飾動詞，形容詞，其他副詞，全句子，子句或片語；但也有例外，可以修飾名詞。

2. 簡單副詞，也稱單字副詞。

    A. 表時間的副詞

        today, tomorrow, now, after, etc.

    B. 表次數的副詞

        once, twic, always, etc.

    C. 表情況的副詞

        quickly, happily, carefully, etc.

    D. 表程度的副詞

        enough, almost, very, etc.

    E. 表肯定或否定的副詞

        no, yes, not, etc.

    F. 表位置，何處的副詞

        everywhere, near, far, around, across, here, where, etc.

3. 疑問副詞

    A. Where-----何地

        a. Where is your school?

        b. Where are your family?

        c. Where is our capital city?

    B. When-----何時

        a. When did you graduate?

        b. When was his birthday?

    c. When are you going to retire?

  C. Who-----何人

    a. Who is your math teacher?

    b. Who can go to the garage with me?

    c. Who are you?

  D. How-----

    a. How are you today?

    b. How is his girl friend?

    c. How did you finish your painting so fast?

4. 關係副詞

  如：how, who, where, when wherever, before, as long as, etc.

    a. The football game will start when the rain stops.

    b. Please put the suitcase wherever you can find a good place.

    c. You may stay my home as long as you like.

5. 副詞的形成

  A. 直接由形容詞加 ly

    如 ： beautiful-----beautifully, kind-----kindly, sudden-----suddenly, stron-----strongly, mad-----madly, etc.

    a. She spoke kindly to her students.

    b. The traffic in the city moves slowly.

  B. 形容詞字尾如為 le 或 e 時，要將 e 去掉再加 ly

    如 ： incredilbe-----incredibly, impossible-----impossibly, simple-----simply, etc.

  C. 形容詞的字尾是主音又加 y 時，要將 y 改成 i 再加 ly

    如 ： heavy-----heavily, busy-----busily, happy-----happily, funny-----funnily, etc.

  D. 有些形容詞和副詞同型，但在意義上會不相同，要看修飾的字

    如：hard-----hard, late-----late, soon-----soon, pretty-----pretty, etc.

    a. The colors aren't <u>fast</u>, so be careful when you wash this shirt.(形容詞)

b. The horse ran <u>fast</u> enough to win the race.(副詞)

c. This question is too <u>hard</u>; I can't answer it.(形容詞)

d. I had to think long and <u>hard</u> before I could find the answer.(副詞)

E. 有些形容詞和副詞加了 ly 之後，仍然是副詞，但是在意義上卻會改變。

如：near-----nearly, hard-----hardly, high-----highly, etc.

F. 如果形容詞的字尾是 ic 時要加 ally 成為副詞

如：basic-----bassically, systematic-----systematically, etc.

但也有例如

如：public-----publicly

6. 副詞的例外

A. 用法的例外——它可以修飾名詞

a. <u>Even</u> a three year old child understand this math.

b. <u>Only</u> Mr. Lee went to the gas station last night.

B. 形狀的例外——字尾有 ly，但它們不是副詞，而是形容詞

a. We have a <u>friendly</u> neighbor.

b. That new couple have a <u>lovely</u> daughter.

c. Mr. Lee is an <u>elderly</u> man.

d. He offered his girlfriend some <u>brotherly</u> advice.

e. John's father gave him a <u>timely</u> decision last night.

f. Mr. Wu is a <u>homely</u> woman with a very kind heart.

C. 名詞的轉用——名詞當副詞用

a. I met Mr. Lee <u>yesterday</u>.

b. You must see your doctor <u>today</u>.

c. After school everybody went <u>home</u>.

7. 有些字可以當副詞也可以當介詞，但是介詞永遠有一個受詞，而副詞卻沒有。

a. We walked <u>along</u> the pier.(介詞)

b. My little brother came <u>along</u>.(副詞)

    c. He swam <u>underneath</u> the dock.(介詞)

    d. He swam <u>underneath</u>.(副詞)

8. 副詞 very 和 too 在意義上有些不同；very 是指某些東西很多，而 too 則是指東西超多，或超過所需。

    a. The car is <u>very</u> long, but it fits into the space.

    b. The weather in Canada is <u>very</u> cold in winter, but Mr. Lee enjoys it very much.

    c. The sun was <u>too</u> hot for the child, and she became sick.

9.副詞的位置

  A. 副詞在它所修飾的字之後

    a. She tiptoed <u>quietly</u>.

    b. She spoke kindly to her <u>students</u>.

    c. He drives <u>carefully</u>.

  B. 副詞在它所修飾的字之前

    a. She <u>seldom</u> finish her homework in class.

    b. She <u>quickly</u> gave him a magic golden bridle.

    c. William, the goddess of wisdom, <u>quickly</u> advised him how to catch the horse.

  C. 副詞在一個句子的最前面修飾全句

    a. <u>Suddenly</u>, we heard a sonic boom.

    b. <u>Surprisingly</u>, more men than women wore wigs in ancient custom.

    c. <u>Certainly</u>, the blacksmith is necessary.

  D. 副詞在一個句子的最後面修飾全句。

    a. I learned some Spanish words <u>quickly</u>.

    b. My little brother crept down the stairs <u>slowly</u>.

    c. A violent storm came up <u>possibly</u>.

  E. 副詞在一個句子的助動詞和主要動詞之間

    a. Vistors to New York can <u>actually</u> experience some aspects of everyday connial life.

b. You would <u>truly</u> enjoy the crafts at New York.

c. He will <u>quickly</u> bait a hook himself.

F. 介詞片語當副詞時，要在所修飾的字旁邊。

a. Our boss left the office <u>without a word</u>.

b. Mr. Lee is happy <u>about his good records</u>.

c. Many new immigrants in Taiwan are satisfied with<u>their health care situation</u>.

G. 副詞子句（從屬子句）當副詞時，要放在句首或句尾，但是標點符號的位置不同。

a. The basketball game will be postponed <u>if it rains</u>.

= <u>If it rains</u>, the basketball game will be postoned.

b. We bought lettuce, tomatoes, and luncheon meats <u>after the baseball game</u>.

= <u>After the baseball game</u>, we bought lettuce, tomatoes, and luncheon meats.

H. 連接副詞通常放在獨立子句與附屬子句之間，但要用分號或用句號做區隔。

a. A storm knocked down our eletric wires; <u>therefore</u>, we had to eat by candlelight.

b. I don't know much about football; <u>accordingly</u>, I can't advise you about it.

c. She was very tired.　Nevertheless, she kept on working.

I. 有些片語可以當連接副詞，這時這些片語，就要放在主要子句和從屬子句之間，但要用分號或句號做區隔。

a. He studies English very hard.　　<u>In addition</u>, he has to study second foreign language.

b. My sister wanted to buy a fur coat; <u>on the other hand</u>, she was trying to save money for a car.

J. 如果一個句子當中有兩個副詞或副詞片語，一個表地方，另外一個表時間，就要將地方副詞放在時間副詞前面，通常也要將較小的放在較大的前面。

 a. The package was placed on the table in the living room. (table 比 room 小)

 b. I have a dental surgeon at 12:30 P.M. next Friday. (at 12:30 P.M.比 next Friday 小)

 c. I watched a Chinese movie in New York last week. (in New York 為地方副詞，要放在時間副詞 last week 之前)

K. 表次數的副詞通常放在主動詞之前，不過卻放在連繫動詞之後。

 a. He always go to work on time.

 b. Did you finnally finish your papers?

 c. Mr. Lee is usually punctual to go to work.

 d. Are you often early to get up?

L. even 和 only 兩個副詞，在一個句子當中，因為擺的位置不同，而產生不同的意義。

 a. Even John knows that 4 and 4 make 8. (雖然他是笨瓜)

 b. John even knows that 4 and 4 make 8. (他知道很多事情)

 c. Only John knows the answer. (沒有人知道，只有 John 知道)

 d. John knows only half of it. (John 只知道一半，其它的不知道)

 e. John only met Jan. (John 只碰到 Jan 沒有別人)

M. 有些字本身就是副詞，因此不需要任何變化，諸如 too, as well, not-----either, and also, etc.副詞 too, as well, not-----either 和 also 的位置通常在肯定句的最後面，如果是否定句時則要將 too 或者 as will 改成 either 但位置不變。

 a. I like John and I like his wife, too.

 b. I like John and I like his wife, as well.

 c. I don't like John and I don't like his wife, either.

N. also 是可以代替 too 和 as well，不過在寫作上較在說話時普遍。

 a.在連繫動詞之後

Sue is an engineer.　She is also a mother.

b.在動詞片語中時則擺在第二個位置

I've written the letters.　I should also have mailed them.

c.在主要動詞之前

I play football and I also play tennis.

O. 表次數的副詞 even 和 never 的使用與擺放的位置。

a. even 的意義是在任何時間，通常在疑問句中使用。

Have you ever thought of applying for a job abroad?

b.我們可以使用 even 在 any-和 no-不確定的代名詞句中。

Does anyone ever visit them?　Nothing ever bothers Mary.

c. even 可以在 if-的肯定句當中。

If you ever need any help, you know where to find me.

d. even 可以跟隨 hardly, scarcely 和 barely 使用。

※ I hardly ever see Tom these days.

※ She scarcely ever spoke a word of English.

※ We have barely ever enough money to last the weekend.

e. never 在否定句中使用，當我們要強調這個否定的語氣時，常常代替 not.

※ I don't smoke.　I never smoke.

f.否定語氣 not-----even 更強調在答應，緊告某件事情時代替 never.

※ I promise you, he won't ever trouble you again.

10. 副詞的比較──原級，比較級和最高級

A.單音節的副詞＋er 成為比較級，＋est 成為最高級。

hard-----harder-----hardest

soon-----sooner-----soonest

often-----oftener-----oftenest

B. 極少數的二音節的副詞也是＋er 成為比較級，＋est 成為最高級。

early-----earlier-----earliest

C. 二音節以上的副詞＋more 成為比較級，＋most 成為最高級。

quick-----more quickly-----most quickly

often-----more often-----most often

pleasantly-----more pleasantly-----most pleasantly

D. 有些副詞的比較級必須加定冠詞 the，但副詞的最高級往往可以將定冠詞 the 省略掉。

a. He is <u>the shortest</u> in this room. (不可省略是形容詞)

He works <u>(the) hardest</u> in Lee's Company.

He ran <u>(the) fastest</u> in that group last week.

b. <u>The sooner</u> you work, <u>the better</u> you will get.

<u>The more</u> money we have, <u>the more</u> food we will buy.

<u>The longer</u> I stay in New York, <u>the less</u> I like that big city.

E. 同等級的比較

a. I go to supermarket as <u>often</u> as Mr. Lee.

b. She walks as <u>slowly</u> as her husband.

c. We can't speak English as <u>well</u> as they.

F. 不同等級的比較——兩者之間

a. I speak English <u>more quickly</u> than my wife.

b. We cut grass <u>more often</u> than our neighbor.

c. Mr. Lee went to work <u>more punctually</u> than Mr. Lin.

G. 不同等級的比較——三者之間

a. William studies <u>(the) most carefully</u> of all students in A class.

b. Class B talk <u>(the) most loudly</u> of whole school.

c. Our teacher wrote <u>(the) most perfectly</u> in our school this year.

11. 只有表示情況的副詞才有互相比較的情形，如果本身已經是有比較的意義時，就不能再做比較。諸如：only, really, extremely, then, daily, there, etc.

a. He can <u>only</u> do his best.

b. Tell me what you <u>really</u> think about it.

c. It is <u>extremely</u> kind of you to invite me.

d. We shall have left school <u>then</u>.

e. Most newspapers appear <u>daily</u>.

f. He will stay <u>there</u> until December.

12. 副詞比較時，不能把自己包括在內，因此要加 anyother, other 或 else.

    a. My brother runs faster than anybody (anyone) <u>else</u> in the game.

    b. John wrote his final paper more carefully than <u>any other</u> student in the clase. (任何一個人)

    c. Tom plays baseball more quickly than <u>other</u> players in the team. (其他人)

第三章 | 介詞 (Prepositions)

1. 介詞是表達名詞與名詞，或名詞，代名詞與其它字之間的關係。

2. 介詞在一個英文句中是非常重要的字，而且也是非常困難了解的字。
   因為不同的介詞在一個句子中就有不同的意義。

   a. I hit the ball over the net.

   I hit the ball into the net.

   b. Your math book is underneath your coat.

   Your math book is behind your coat.

   c. The driver behind us honked his horn.

   The driver beside us honked his horn.

3. 簡單介詞——為了徹底了解各個介詞的功能以及與其它介詞比較時有
   何不同，可以利用下列四種圖形：

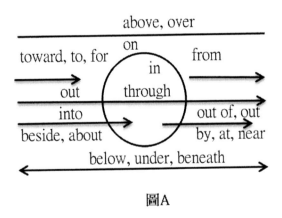

圖A

   a. Sometimes I walk to work.

   b. I always eat in the cafeteria.

   c. I had only a sandwich for lunch.

d. That is a large map on th wall.

e. I get up at six o'clock every morning.

f. Tell me all about your trip to Washington, D.C.

g. We flew above the clouds.

h. The shop is open from eight till five o'clock.

i. The dog jumped over the fence.

j. The plane fell into the river.

k. Is silver Spring near Washington, D.C. or far from it?

l. The temperature dropped from ten degress above zero to ten degrees below zero.

m. The elevator is out of order today.

n. Her English is improving little by little.

o. He went out the main door.

p. Come and stand beside me.

q. She pushed her way through the crowd.

r. What are you wearing under the coat?

s. We live beneath the same roof.

t. He was walking toward (towards) the park.

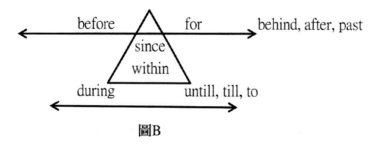

圖B

a. January always comes before February.

b. The child ran and tried to hide behind the tree.

c. She will be in Europe for six months.

d. She has worked in that office since last year.

e. We'll have to postpone our trip until next month.

f. He swins every day during the summer.

g. He did not return till ten o'clock.

h. They'll arrived at home within a week.

i. He walked past the gate.

j. It is twenty-five past ten.

k. It is twelve to eleven.

l. He toiled day after day without a word of complaint.

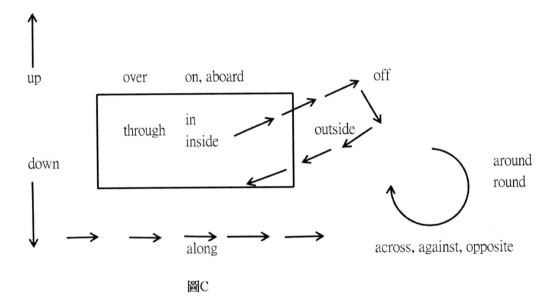

圖C

a. I write all the new words in my notebook

b. Yesterday Judy paid my fare on the bus.

c. He wants to take a trip around the world.

d. We climbed up a ladder to the roof.

e. They sailed down a stream yesterday.

f. The troops marched through the town.

g. Those people work under a famous scientist.

h. He put the newspaper over his face.

i. Keep off the grass.

j. The rain beat against the window.

k. Trees grew along the river bank.

l. They live across the road from us.

m. They built a fence round the house.

n. He has never been aboard a ship.

o. There are a lot of subway stations inside the buildings in the United States.

p. He was standing and talking with his friend just outside the door.

q. Your school is just opposite our house.

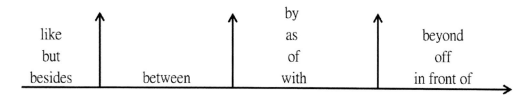

圖D

a. What is the opposite of the word pull?

b. The teacher stands in front of the class.

c. What is the difference between those two words?

d. She will be very angry with you.

e. Their house is hidden among trees.

f. The fruit tree is beyond my reach.

g. He offered me the goods at 20% off the regular price.

h. As a writer she's excellent, but as a teacher she's not very good.

i. No one answered the teacher's question but (except) me.

j. Besides his parents and himself, everyone believed that he was too young to drive a taxicab.

k. The mouse was killed by him with a stone.

l. I'll go to New York by train next week.

m. That blind man can't walk without a stick.

n. He picked up some small hard things like stones.

4. 雙重介詞——兩個介詞在句子中連著用，嚴格來說，通常介詞要有受詞，而副詞不需要受詞。因此前面的介詞應屬於副詞，而後面的一個才是真正的介詞。

   a. She pulled the chair out from under the table.

   b. Mr. Johnson waited till after dark.

5. 片語介詞（或稱複合介詞）兩個介詞或兩個介詞加上名詞組合而成。諸如：

ahead of, apart from, because of, in addition to, in front of, in regard to, in spite of, on top of, owing to, prior to, according to, apart from, as of, aside from, by means of, in the name of, in back, in case of, in place of, instead of, in view of, on account of, out of with a view to, etc.

   a. A big bus is ahead of my car.

   b. Apart from being smart, our first lady is kind and beautiful.

   c. Because of a staff shortage, all trains are running late.

   d. I'm slow but I'm in front of you.

6. 介詞片語——介詞加上它的受詞構成介詞片語。

   A. 當形容詞用（也可以稱為形容詞片語）

      a. Some boys in the school have formed a basketball team.

      b. She dumped more leaves on the huge pile.

      c. I received a letter from my aunt and uncle.

      d. Do you have the answer to the last question?

   B. 當副詞用（也可以稱為副詞片語）

      a. Please drive with care.   It's a rainy day.

      b. I went to New York by train last week.

      c. In his spare time, our father wandered through the woods.

7. 介詞的受詞

介詞一定要有一個受詞，而受詞則有名詞，代名詞，動名詞，名詞片語和名詞子句等等。

a. That big tree is behind our house. (名詞)

b. I sit in front of him in the class. (代名詞)

c. My younger brother insisted on going finishing. (動名詞)

d. I really don't know about how to finish that job. (名詞片語)

e. Tomorrow's picnic depends on whether it'll rain or not. (名詞子句)

8. 介詞與副詞的區別

介詞只是片語介詞或介詞片語的一部分，因此有其受詞，而副詞則獨立使用並無受詞。

a. I came aboard the skiff. (介詞)

I came aboard. (副詞)

b. He swam underneath the dock. (介詞)

He swam underneath. (副詞)

c. We walked along the pier. (介詞)

My little brother came along. (副詞)

9. 介詞的位置

A. 單字介詞通常要放在受詞之前。

a. The man in the black high boots walks slowly.

b. A brief of World War I is in the first chapter.

c. A large crowd walked up the stairs in the historic building.

d. Surprised by the house owner's return, the intruder hurried through the door.

e. The unseasoned traveler put his hand into his pocket.

f. The book on the top shelf belongs to Adam.

g. After more peaceful methods had failed, the government seized control of the newspapers and radio stations.

h. Combined with the bank's inter-office banking service is their policy of all-day, all-night depositing.

i. In dull winter weather, African violets will bloom under 100 watt grow lights.

j. Sitting beside me was a man who laughed and clapped loudly.

k. The unfortunate children were scattered among many homes.

B. 單字介詞如果在下列情況時，要放在句子的最後面。

　　a. These children must be taken care of. (動詞片語在被動式時)

　　b. Where did those tourers come from? (受詞為疑問詞時)

　　c. There is no room to move in. (位於不定詞作形容詞用之後時)

　　d. It is the dog that we have been looking for. (受詞為關係代名詞時)

C. 介詞片語當形容詞片語用時，通常要放在被形容字的旁邊，如果當成副詞片語時，可以放在句首（有強調的意味），也可以放在句尾（較弱的意味）

　　a. The fire in the fireplace crackled into the night.

　　b. The dentist's ultrasonic cleaner sped along the surfaces of the patient's teeth.

　　c. Druing the training session, the recruits crawled under the fence.

　　d. The dealer dividend the cards among the four players.

　　e. Despite their increasing representation in the work force, the income of women has failed to spproch that of men.

　　f. The boss finally finished the project with the assistance of his loyal and helpful employees.

　　g. On its way, Galileo flew through a powerful dust storm.

　　h. Shrubbery grew around the house.

　　i. A contestant with a soprano voice won the talent competition.

　　j. A lonely figure waited on the bridge.

　　k. Everyone except him cheered.

　　l. A brief summary is in the first chapter.

　　m. A large crowd walked up the stairs in the historic building.

　　n. Surprised by the house owner's return, the intruder hurried through the door.

D. 片語介詞的位置在句首，句中或句尾都有可能，就要看句子中那一個字，那一個片語，甚至那一個子句與其最密切就要儘量靠近。

a. We don't know many people in this community aside from the Lees.

b. In case of rain, take the umbrella for yourself.

c. The storm was furious, and the ship was beneath the lee of a harbor.

d. I gave him twenty dollars over and above the amount agreed to.

e. Outside of his secretary, no one knows his views.

f. This event was prior to the war.

g. We knew that news according to today's newspaper.

h. Our big problem is ahead of us.

i. Aside from his salary, he has no extra money for his rental.

j. You will know the fact by and by.

k. He has finished his homework by means of his industry.

第四章　名詞（Nouns）

1. 名詞是告訴我們人，事，地及某種動植物等的名稱。此外，很多名詞是用在限定字之後，諸如 a, the, this 等等，以及常與其它字接合構成名詞片語。名詞或名詞片語來回答 who, what 或下列情形：

　A.　當動詞的主詞

　　a. Our agent in Boston sent a telex this afternoon.

　　　（Our agent 是主詞，sent 是動詞）

　　b. I watched a TV show last night.

　　　（I 是主詞，watched 是動詞）

　B.　當動詞的直接受詞

　　a. Mary sent an urgent telex from Washington, D.C. this morning.

　　　（telex 是直接受詞，sent 是動詞）

　　b. He wrote a long sentence fro his homework.

　　　（sentence 是直接受詞，wrote 是動詞）

　C.　當動詞的間接受詞

　　a. Frank sent his boss a telex from France.

　　　（his boss 是間接受詞，sent 是動詞）

　　b. John built his dog a good room.

　　　（his dog 是間接受詞，built 是動詞）

　D.　當介詞的受詞

　　a. I read my boss's scandal in the newspaper.

　　　（in 是介詞，the newspaper 是受詞）

　　b. Washington, D.C. is the capital of the United States of America.

　　　（of 是介詞，the United States of America 是受詞）

E.當做 be 動詞或相關動詞如 seam 之類的補語。

　　a. Uncle Lee is our guest today.

　　　(is 是 be 動詞之一，our guest 是補語)

　　b. It seems to me that it will be a problem.

　　　(seems 是動詞，to me 是補語)

F.當做同位語

　　a. Rong Chen, an NBC reporter, asked for an interview.

　　　(Rong Chen 和 an NBC reporter 是指同一個人)

　　b. English, a foreign language, used in the world long long time.

　　　(English 和 a foreign language 是指同件事物)

G.當做我們直接提及的某個人

　　a. Wilson, close that window, will you please?

　　　(Wilson 是直接被提及的人)

　　b. John, don't touch the fire.

　　　(John 是直接被提及的人)

2. 可數名詞

　可以分單、複數的名詞（可以看得到或摸得到的具體東西）。

　A. 普通名詞

　　如：table; chair, book, pen, candy, country, banana, hat, cap, etc.

　　a. There are a lot of bananas in the market. (bananas 是普通名詞)

　　b. How many chairs and tables are in our classroom?

　　　(chairs 和 tables 是普通名詞)

　　c. We bought some garlice in this morning. (garlice 是普通名詞)

　B. 集合名詞

　　指一個群體（人或動植物）當做一個單位，是單數。

　　如：people, family, council, team, band, staff, etc.

　　a. That family is our good neighbor. (family 是集合名詞)

　　b. Our state council has a big power. (council 是集合名詞)

　　c. The big jury has reached a verdict. (jury 是集合名詞)

3. 不可數名詞

因為不能數它們的數量，所以無單、複數之別。

A. 專有名詞——人名，地名和國名等等。

如：China, Taiwan, New York, Japan, Boston, etc.

a. We live in Taipei. (Taipei 為專有名詞)

b. My grand son studies at Blair High School in Maryland. (Blair High School 和 Maryland 均為專有名詞)

c. Our country is the Republic of China. (the Republic of China 是專有名詞)

B. 物質名詞——指自然界中各種物質。

如：air, water, gold, silver, iron, etc.

a. Air is necessary for our life. (air 是物質名詞)

b. My ring is made of gold. (gold 是物質名詞)

c. Silver is very expensive material. (Silver 是物質名詞)

C. 抽象名詞——指感官上無法察覺，而且看不到也摸不到的物質。

如：justice, fear, success, health, honesty, knowledge, ability, etc

a. Justice is very important in the world. (justice 是抽象名詞)

b. The people fight for freedom everywhere. (freedom 是抽象名詞)

c. Don't worry about failure, you need try it again and again. (failure 是抽象名詞)

4. 複合名詞

名詞加上一個或兩個以上的字，接連在一起，指一個人或一件事。

A. 每個字分開的複合名詞

如：dog days of sumber, fruit cake, senior high school, post office, police station, boarding gate, etc.

a. The landing gear of Boing 747 is so huge. (landing gear 是複合名詞)

b. If you climb the mountain, you need a pair of jump suit. (jump suit 是複合名詞)

c. The mail man delivers letters six days a week. (mail man 是複合名

詞）

B. 每個字是用連字號連在一起的複合名詞。

如：father-in-law, mother-in-law, commander-in-chief, etc.

a. My father-in-law past away long time ago.

(father-in-law 是複合名詞)

b. We got a new commander-in-chief recently.

(commander-in-chief 是複合名詞)

c. My sister-in-law went to Japan last month.

(sister-in-law 是複合名詞)

C. 兩個字連在一起成為一個字的複合名詞

如：firefighter, eyewitness, chairperson, housekeeper, etc.

a. This lady is our neighbor's housekeeper.

(housekeeper 是複合名詞)

b. We are very satisfied to get a good bookkeeper.

(bookkeeper 是複合名詞)

c. The lawmaker of the U.S.A. is very powerful.

(lawmaker 是複合名詞)

5. 字本身為集合名詞不用複數，但意義上每個分開來時，卻是普通名詞，有單、複數之別。

如：food, homework, money, etc.

a. He has a lot of food in his refrigerator.

(food 為集合名詞，但包括 apples, oranges, pineapples, vegetables, etc.就有單、複之分)

b. Mr. Wang has a big family.

(family 為集合名詞，grand-father, grand-mother, father, mother, etc. 這些成員就有單、複之分)

c. Our committee just approved a new project last month.

(committee 為集合名詞，但包括很多男女委員，因此 menbers 就有單、複之分)

6. 字形為複數型，但意義上卻為單數名詞。

    a. No news is a good news. (news 為單數名詞)

    b. Do you think electronics is more difficult than mathematics?

      (electronics 和 mathematics 均為單數名詞)

    c. We know arthritis is very terrible disease. (arthritis 為單數名詞)

7. 集合名詞有關人或事物當做單一，但強調各個成員時，動詞要用複數。

    a. After the plans are completed, the committee are going their homes.

      (committee 為集合名詞，are 為複數動詞)

    b. This jury are twelve men and women.

      (jury 為集合名詞，are 為複數動詞)

8. 集合名詞強調一個團體時，就要用單數動詞。

    a. The committe is planning its work carefully.

    (committee 為集合名詞，is 為單數動詞)

    b. The jury has decided that the prisoner is guilty.

    (jury 為集合名詞，has decided 為單數動詞)

9. 集合名詞雖然沒有複數型態，卻要用複數動詞。

    a. Some people are never satisfied.

    b. The police have surrounded the building.

    c. These cattle are from Holland.

    d. The clergy have a lot of power in some countries.

    e. The military keep order in the city right now.

    f. Some swine are white, but some swine are black.

    g. Those vermin are very harmful to plants or animals.

10. 可數名詞和不可數名詞的區別

    A. 可數名詞

    a. 我們可以使用 a 或 an 在它的前面。

    ※This is a new book on the table.

    ※There is an envelop in my drawer.

b. 我們可以使用數字在它的前面。

※We have <u>one pear</u> left today.

※We have <u>two pears</u> left today.

B. 不可數名詞

　　a. 我們不能使用 a 或 an 在它的前面。

　　※<u>Sugar</u> is necessary to our body. (正確)

　　※<u>A sugar</u> is necessary to our body. (錯誤)

　　b. 通常沒有複數型，而且只能用在 how much 的問句中。

　　※<u>How much meat</u> do you want? (正確)

　　※I want a lot of <u>meats</u>. (錯誤)

　　※I just want a piece of <u>meat</u>. (正確)

　　※I just want a <u>meat</u>. (錯誤)

　　c. 我們不能使用數字在它前面。

　　※There is <u>a cup of coffee</u> on the table. (正確)

　　※There is <u>one coffee</u> on the table. (錯誤)

　　※There are <u>two bottles of water</u> left at home. (正確)

　　※There are <u>two waters</u> left at home. (錯誤)

11. 同位語

兩個或兩個以上的名詞片語同時發生，且彼此指同一個人或同一件事，它們被稱為同位語。

A. 同位語可以互換位置

　　a. <u>A neighbor of yours</u>, <u>William Lee</u>, will be visiting us this evening.

　　b. <u>William Lee</u>, <u>a neighbor of yours</u>, will be visiting us this evening.

B. 同位語之間的關係是表達主詞和它的補語是指同一個。

　　a. <u>William Lee</u> is <u>a neighbor of yours</u>.

　　b. <u>A neighbor of yours</u> is <u>William Lee</u>.

C. 我們能夠認為第二個同位語的要素是省略的非限定關係子句中要加點號。它們提供了額外的而且可以省略的資訊。

　　a. <u>William Lee</u>, (who is) <u>a neighbor of yours</u>, will be visiting us this evening.

    b. <u>A neighbor of yours</u>, (who is) <u>William Lee</u>, will be visiting us this evening.

  D. 當第一個要素限定第二個要素，而且沒有點號時的關係子句中，限定同位語就非常重要。因為它們提供了主詞或受詞基本的訊息。

    a. <u>Mr. Lee</u>, <u>our English teacher</u>, is very kind.

    你認為是那一位 Mr. Lee?

    Mr. Lee 是 teacher?還是 lawyer?

    b. <u>My good friend</u> <u>Bob</u> is going to study in college next spring.

12. 動名詞是動詞＋ing 而來，它是名詞因此可以當做主詞或受詞

    a. The man was given a ticket for <u>driving the wrong way on a one-way-street</u>. (受詞)

    b. <u>Smoking</u> is not allowed on the bus. (主詞)

    c. <u>Shouting</u> at people does not make them understand you better. (主詞)

    d. My favorite sport is <u>boating</u>. (受詞)

13. 動名詞是名詞，因此任何名詞或代名詞，緊接在它之前要用所有格。

    a. The vultures didn't let anything disturb <u>their</u> feeding.

    b. The blue <u>jay's</u> screeching at the cat woke us at dawn.

14. 動名詞可以為現在式，也可以為完成式。

  A. 被用在現在式時，是它的行動與主動詞的行動在同時發生。

    a. <u>Flying</u> is the fastest and the most convenient to get abroad.

    b. <u>Taking</u> driving lessons will help you drive better.

    c. My brother <u>singing</u> in the shower adds mirth and music to our morning routine.

  B. 動名詞被用在完成式時，是它的行動全部完成在主動詞之前。

    a. I am ashamed of <u>having done</u> that mistake.

    b. He believes his success is a result of his <u>having studied</u> hard.

    c. Our <u>having read</u> the novel made the movie boring.

15. 名詞的所有格是指所有者是誰。

    A. 不管是人或活的東西的所有，均用省略符號 "'" 加上 s 來表示。

        a. <u>Paul's</u> father wants him to help paing the house.

        b. The <u>squirrel's</u> tail is very long.

        c. There are fifteen <u>teacher's</u> room in my school.

        d. Many <u>children's</u> toys will be sold in Christmas season.

        e. My <u>father-in-law's</u> house is near the countryside.

        f. Somebody <u>else's</u> umbrella left on the bus.

        g. <u>My daughter and my son's</u> school is located on 14th street. (一個學校)

        h. My <u>father's and my mother's</u> cars are different colors. (兩部車)

        i. I'm going to the <u>barber's</u> (or barber's shop) tomorrow night.

        j. His youngest son doesn't like to go to the <u>dentist's</u> (or dentist's office).

        k. Your house is bigger than your <u>sister's</u> (or sister's house).

    B. 有生命的或沒有生命的都有可能使用 "of" 片語來表示。也可以用 "'" 省略符號加 "s" 來表示。

        a. The leg <u>of</u> the desk is broken.

        b. Washington, D.C. is the capital <u>of</u> the United States of America.

        c. Did you read <u>today's</u> newspaper?

        d. A <u>dollar's</u> worth of sugar was stolen last night.

        e. Who cut the tail <u>of</u> that dog?

        f. Would you like to spend three <u>month's</u> journey?

    C. "of" 片語和雙重所有格，在正式英文裡常被使用在無生命的事物擁有某種東西時，或避免拙的構句中。

        a. He is the best friend <u>of</u> my <u>brother's</u>.

        b. The passage <u>of</u> the bill now in Congress will mean lower tapes.

        c. The mother <u>of</u> my <u>brother-in-law's</u> uncle is ninety-three years old.

16. 名詞由單數變成複數的規則。

    A. 絕大多數的單數名詞，不管最後字母發音或不要發音加上 "s" 就

　　形成複數名詞。如果單數名詞的字展為 s, sh, ch, x 或 z 就加上
　　"es" 形成複數名詞。

　　如：hen-----hens, church-----churches, box-----boxes

B. 如果筆數名詞的字尾為 f 或 fe 將 f 或 fe 改成 v 再加上 es 就形成複
　　數名詞。但有些單數名詞的字尾為 f 加上 s 或 es 均可成為複數名
　　詞。

　　如：wife-----wives, chief-----chiefs, hoof-----hoofs 或 hooves

C. 如果單數名詞的字尾為 y 而且它的前面為子音時，應將 y 改成 i 再
　　加 es；如果它的前面為母音時，則加 s 即可成為複數名詞。

　　如：sky-----skies, monkey-----monkeys

D. 有些單數名詞要變成複數名詞，不是加上 s 或 es，而是它們的拼法
　　改變。

　　如：woman-----women, mouse-----mice, goose-----geese

E. 有些單數名詞字尾為 o，而它的前面為子音時，加上 es 成為複數
　　名詞；如果它的前面為母音時，加上 s 即可成為複數名詞。

　　如： potato-----potatoes, tomato-----tomatoes, radio-----radios, zoo-
　　zoos.

F. 有些單數名詞和複數名詞拼法相同，但在使用上和意義上卻是單
　　數。不過有些名詞仍然被當做複數在使用。

　　如：sheep-----sheep, ashes-----ashes

　　measles 和 civics 兩個字均為複數型態，但是在使用上為單甦。而
　　shoes 和 scissors 為複數型態，但在使用上仍然為複數。

G. 連字號的複數名詞型態通常在主要字之上，有時候母音在另外一
　　部分時，則在那個字加上 s 形成複數名詞。

　　如：brother-in-law-----brothers-in-law, manservant-----menservants

H. 如果單數名詞的字尾為 ful 時，它們的字尾加上 s 即形成複數名
　　詞。

　　如：cupful-----cupfuls, handful-----handfuls

I. 通常數字和字母加上 s 就形成複數名詞。假如加上 s 形成意義上不

　　清楚時，則需加上省略符號 "," 之後再加 s。

　　如：1950-----1950s, a-----a's

　J. 名詞如引用外國字時，仍然保持它們的複數型態。

　　如：alummus-----alumni, alumna-----alumnae

17. 基數為 one, two, three, etc.而序數則為 the first, the second, the third, etc. 基數之前不可以加 the，也不可以在名詞之後加基數。

　　a. Independence Day in the United States is the fourth of July.

　　b. Our teacher just taught us Chapter five of history.

　　c. Many people were killed in World War II (Two).

18. 單數名詞變成複數名詞的更多例子。

　　a. office-----offices, pin-----pins, fox-----foxes, dish-----dishes

　　b. leaf-----leaves, half-----halves, loaf-----loaves, knife-----knives

　　c. baby-----babies, country-countries, story-----stories

　　d. child-----children, foot-----feet, die-----dice, person-----people, ox-----oxes

　　e. veto-----vetoes, two-----twos, solo-----solos, hero-----heroes

　　f. deer-----deer, species-----species, corp-----corps

　　g. 　lady-in-waiting-----ladies-in-waiting, 　attorney-in-general-----attorneys-in-general

　　h. datum-----data, phenomenon-----phenomena, crisis-----crises

19. 不可數名詞的數量，可以用下列方法來計算。

　　a. 用形數表示

　　如：a bar of soap, an ear of corn, a slice of bread, a piece of cake, etc.

　　b. 用容器表示

　　如：a bottle of water, a cup of coffee, two cartons of milk, three glasses of water, etc.

　　c. 用重量或容量表示

　　如：a pound of meat, a gallon of milk, two ounces of sugar, etc.

20. 不可數名詞有時也可做可數名詞。

a. Iron is a very important material about construction. (不可數)

We use irons to press our T-shirts all the time. (可數)

b. Knowledge is very powerful. (不可數)

We learned a lot of knowledges from that case. (可數)

21. 不可數名詞如果數量很多時用 much, too much 或 a lot of。數量很少時用 little, a little 或 very little 來表示。

a. He has much homework to do this Sunday.

b. Nobody says he has too much money.

c. Don't worry we have a lot of time to go to the train station.

d. We have little sugar left so far.

e. We just need a little milk for our breakfast.

f. Hurry up you have very little time to take your exam.

22. 可數名詞數量很少時可用 few, a few 和 too few 來表示。

a. He has few friends at school.

b. A few pages of this book are broken.

c. They have too few people to move that big stone away from the small road.

23. 可數名詞如果用 much, many, a lot of, a little, a few 來表示時，有「很多」或「有一些」的意思。如果用 too much, too many, too little, too few 來表示時，卻有「太多」或「有不多」之意。

a. He is busy, because he has too much work. (正確)

He is not busy, because he has too much work. (錯誤)

b. She is succeed, because he has a lot of experience. (正確)

She is not succeed, because she has a lot of experience. (錯誤)

24. 名詞的單數與複數意義上不相同。

a. work (工作)-----works (工廠)

b. cloth (布料)-----clothes (衣服)

c. manner (樣子)-----manners (態度)

d. glass (玻璃)-----glasses (玻璃杯，眼鏡)

25. 名詞的性別與轉換

A. 性別種類

a. 雄性-----father, boy, tiger, etc.

b. 雌性-----mother, girl, tigress, etc.

c. 中性-----teacher, friend, student, etc.

d. 無性-----house, pencil, bridge, etc.

B. 性別轉換

a. 字尾加 "ess"

actor-----actress; host-----hostess; waiter-----waitress; lion-----lioness, etc.

b. 加一個字或改一個字

boy-scout-----girl-scout; father-in-law-----mother-in-law; he-goat----- she-goat, etc.

C. 完全改變不同字

male-----female; son-----daughter; cock-----hen; brother-----sister, etc.

26. 所有格之後名詞的省略

A. 有一個句子中，第二次使用同一名詞時可將其省略，否則重複使用太不簡潔。

a. This beautiful night gown is Mary's (night gown).

b. My house is bigger than your's (house).

B. 所有格後面的特定名詞也可以省略。

a. My friend was staying at his (house, school, etc.).

b. I'm going to the barber's (shop) this afternoon.

27. 有些英文字，如 this, that, no, a, which, any, etc.與有生命的名詞所有格共同修飾同一個名詞時，必須使用雙重所有格，否則會造成語意不清晰。

a. This book of my sister's is very expensive. (正確)

This book of my sister is very expensive. (錯誤)

My sister's this book is very expensive. (錯誤)

This my sister's book is very expensive. (錯誤)

b. Any student of Mr. Armstrong's is male. (正確)

Any student of Mr. Armstrong is male. (錯誤)

Mr. Armstrong's any student is male. (錯誤)

c. A movie of American's is very interesting. (正確)

A movie of American is very interesting. (錯誤)

American's a movie is very interesting. (錯誤)

An American's movie is very interesting. (錯誤)

28. 名詞的性與代名詞的關係

A. 雄性用 he, his, him 為其代名詞。

a. A man is writing his paper and the boy is reading.

b. He is a father of three kids.

c. Do you like your grand-father?

Yes, I like him.

B. 雌性用 she, her 為其代名詞。

a. She is a very kind lady.

b. Her hari is the longest in this room.

c. Do you told her about that accident?

C. 中性或無性的名詞用 it 為它們的代名詞。

a. This stone is very big and heavy.　Please move it away carefully.

b. Don't too close that dog.　It is very dangerous.

c. This is a good insect.　Don't kill it.

D. 將有些名詞擬人化時，強壯的或可怕的事物當做雄性；而弱小的或可愛的當做雌性。

a. Your puppy is very cute.　she or he. (female or male)

b. Don't bother the tiger!　He is a very fierce animal.

c. Everybody likes spring, because she is mild.

第五章 │ 代名詞（pronouns）

1. 代名詞顧名思義，就是代替名詞的詞。因為這樣，在一個英文句中，甚至一般英文一篇文章內，都用相同名詞的現象才可避免。如此一來，不管在演講或寫作才會生動而有趣。

2. 代名詞所代替的名詞，我們稱為先行詞。

   A. 先行詞的數、格和性必須與代名詞一致。

   a. My Aunt Judy sold her car last summer. (Judy 是 her 的先行詞)

   b. John call his father. (John 是 his 的先行詞)

   c. The dentist washed her hands before examining my mouth. (dentist 是 her 的先行詞)

   d. Our aunt and uncle have decided that they will visit Japan this winter. (aunt 和 uncle 是 they 的先行詞)

   e. Infants cannot take care of themselves. (infants 是 themselves 的先行詞)

   f. Mr. Lee emigrated his family from Taiwan to the U.S.A. long time ago. (Mr. Lee 是 his 的先行詞)

   B. 但例外的是，代名詞有可能沒有先行詞。

   a. Who will speech at school? (who 為代名詞無先行詞)

   b. Everybody is dangerous in the hurricane. (everybody 為代名詞但無先行詞)

3.　人稱代名詞的格，數和性列表如下：

人稱	格		主格	所有格	受格
第一人稱	單數		I	my, mine	me
	複數		We	our, ours	us
第二人稱	單數		you	your, yours	you
	複數		you	your, yours	you
第三人稱	單數		he, she, it	his, her, here, its	him, her, it
	複數		they	their, theirs	them

a. Dad told the mechanics to call <u>him</u> to let <u>him</u> know how much his bill would be.

b. <u>Our</u> aunt and uncle have decided that <u>they</u> will visit Greece this spring.

c. <u>You</u> gave <u>us</u> <u>your</u> support when <u>we</u> needed <u>it</u>.

d. This jacket is <u>mine</u>; that one must be <u>yours</u> or his.

e. Is <u>your</u> or <u>her</u> dog losing <u>its</u> hair?

f. The brand-new car is <u>theirs</u>; <u>it</u> has many desirable features, such as automatic overdrive and a near-window defroster.

g. <u>We</u> peeled the potatoes but forgot to add <u>them</u> to the stew, so <u>it</u> wasn't as good as usual.

4.　反身代名詞的格，數和性列表如下：

第一人稱	單數	I-----myself
	複數	We-----ourselves
第二人稱	單數	you-----yourself
	複數	you-----yourselfves
第三人稱	單數	he-----himself it-itself she-----herself
	複數	they-----themselves

a. Infants cannot take care of <u>themselves</u>.

b. Judy can help <u>herself</u> to do a lot of business.

c. She asked me for a picture of <u>myself</u>.

d. Did you ever ask <u>yourself</u> "why"?

e. He cut <u>himself</u> in the kitchen.

f. The battery recharges <u>itself</u>.

5. 指示代名詞，如 this (these), that (those)等等。this 和 these 指比較近的，而 that 和 those 指比較遠的。指示代名詞可放在先行詞的前面或後面。

   a. This is the library I go to very often. (指示代名詞 this 放在先行詞 library 的前面)

   b. I need to mop all chairs in the living room; those are too much dust. (指示代名詞 those 放在先行詞 chairs 之後)

6. 關係代名詞

   連接句子中附屬子句和主要子句之用。

   如：which, that, whose, who, whom, etc.

   a. Here is the clock that I want to set. (that 為連接詞，here is the clock 為主要子句，而 that I want to set 為附屬子句)

   b. The young man whom you talk last week is my sister's boy friend. (whom 為代名詞，the young man is my sister's boy friend 為主要子句，whom you talk last week 為附屬子句)

   c. The woman <u>who</u> wrote this letter works in a hospital.

   d. A snorkel is a hollow tube <u>that</u> lets a diver breathe underwater.

   e. Jefferson, <u>whose</u> property included stables as well as farm fields, went horseback riding at noon.

   f. Afterward, he ate breakfast, <u>which</u> was served promptly at 8:30A.M.

7. 疑問代名詞

   what, which, who, whose 和 whom, etc.均可為疑問代名詞，which 有先行詞，其餘的多半沒有先行詞。

   a. What do you mean?

(what 為疑問代名詞，沒有先行詞，沒有指定什麼東西)

    b. Which is the best reason to your coming late.

    (which 為疑問代名詞，reason 為其先行詞)

8. 不定代名詞

對於人，地，事物或理想等等無特定指那一個，有時也沒有先行詞。

A. 指單數的不定代名詞

    如：another, anyone, each, either, no one, one, everyone, something, etc.

    a. Anyone can decide to vote in the committee election. (Anyone 為不定代名詞，沒有先行詞)

    b. Listen!　No one can leave this classroom. (No one 為不定代名詞，沒有先行詞)

    c. Each of these apples has been rotten. (Each 為不定代名詞，筆數動詞)

    d. Each of the freshmen was welcome to the party.

    e. No one understands a person who mumbles.

    f. Someone among the store owners donates the trophy each year.

    g. Someone in the class left his (or her) pencil. (單數代名詞)

    h. Anyone can join if he (or she) collects stamps. (單數代名詞)

    i. Anybody can improve his (or her) writing with practice. (單數代名詞)

B. 指多數的不定代名詞

    如：few, others, both, etc.

    a. Few are going to market weekdays. (few 是複數不定代名詞，沒有先行詞)

    b. This cat is male and others are female. (others 是複數不定代名詞，有先行詞 cat)

    c. Both are students. (Both 為不定代名詞，有先行詞 students)

    d. Few of them are any good.

    e. She and her husband both like dancing.

C. 可指多數或單數的不定代詞

如：all, some, any, etc.

a. <u>All</u> of us <u>are</u> married in this group. (All 為多數不定代名詞)

<u>All</u> of the money <u>was</u> stolen last night. (All 為單數不定代名詞)

b. <u>Some</u> of cups <u>are</u> broken. (Some 為多數不定代名詞)

<u>Some</u> water <u>is</u> necessary for these flowers. (Some 為單數不定代名詞)

c. There are 10 new students this semester? Are there <u>any</u>?

(any 為多數不定代名詞)

I need some sugar for this soup.　Do you have <u>any</u>?

(any 為單數不定代名詞)

d. <u>All</u> of the nation's interest <u>enters</u> on politics during a political convention. (單數)

e. <u>All</u> of the states <u>send</u> delegates to national political conventions. (複數)

f. <u>Some</u> of the excitement of such a convention <u>is</u> conveyed by television coverage. (單數)

g. <u>Some</u> of the delegates <u>are</u> disappointed in the candidate who is chosen. (複數)

9. 每一個代名詞必須言及它的先行詞，否則在一個句子中意義會不清楚。因此代名詞的使用要遵行下列三個原則：

A. 不可使用兩個名詞當做先行詞。

B. 不可使用 which, this 或 that 說明整個思想。

C. 不可使用人稱代名詞 you, they, them 或 it 等等，除非它們談論特定的名詞。

a. Mary told Nancy that <u>she</u> was very tired. (錯誤，指誰不明)

Mary told Nancy, "<u>You</u> are very tired." (正確，you 是指 Nancy)

Mary told Nancy, "<u>I</u> am very tired." (正確，I 是指 Mary)

b. My younger brother always challenges everything I say, <u>which</u>

unnerves me. (錯誤，意義不明)

My younger brother always challenges everything I say, <u>a habit which</u> unnerves me. (正確，是指 a habit)

    c. My cousin is bad at tennis because he can't hit <u>them</u> across the net. (錯誤，意義不明)

My cousin is bad at tennis because he can't hit <u>the balls</u> across the net. (正確，是指球)

10. 代名詞的先行詞在數，性和格上必須一致。

    a. The dentist washed her hands before examining my mouth.

(先行詞 dentist 和代名詞 her 一致)

    b. The passengers waved to their friends on shore.

(先行詞 passengers 和代名詞 their 一致)

    c. Each of the girls in the class has offered her ideas.

(先行詞 girls 和代名詞 each 及 her 一致)

    d. Everyone of the parents praised his or her child's efforts.

(代名詞 everyone, his 和 her 一致)

11. 用反身代名詞去代替受格的代名詞並不是正常的用法。

    a. He gave the new TV to <u>me</u> yesterday. (正確)

He gave the new TV to <u>myself</u> yesterday. (錯誤)

    b. They built that bridge for <u>us</u> ten years ago. (正確)

They built that bridge for <u>ourselves</u> ten years ago. (錯誤)

12. 當人身代名詞為主詞時，I, you, he, she, it, we 和 they 必須為主格的形式。

    a. He and she sat in the shade. (He 和 she 均為主格)

    b. You and I have been friends for a long time. (you and I 均為主格)

    c. Are you and they going to the basketball game? (you and they 均為主格)

13. 當先行詞的主格在句子中為代名詞時，要小心的使用那個代名詞為主詞的形態。

a. The first speakers might be <u>he</u> and <u>I</u>. (he 和 I 的為主格)

b. On the team, the fastest runners are <u>we</u> three boys. (we 為主格)

c. It might have been <u>I</u> near the drinking fountain. (I 為主格)

14. 一個代名詞如果被用做直接受詞或間接受詞時，一律要用受格的形態。

a. The neighbors hired John and <u>us</u> to rake their yard. (us 為受格)

b. The usher showed Judy and <u>them</u> to their seats. (them 為受格)

c. Why don't you sing <u>her</u> a lullaby? (her 為受格)

15. 一個代名詞如果被用做介詞的受詞時要用受格的形態。當介詞之後有兩個或兩個以上代名詞時，每一個都要使用受格的形態。

a. Just between <u>you</u> and <u>me</u>, that game wasn't much fun. (you 和 me 均為受格)

b. If you have a complaint, tell it to Mr. Lee or her. (<u>Mr. Lee</u> 和 <u>her</u> 均為受格)

16. 兩個或兩個以上的先行詞用 "or" 連接時，必須用單數代名詞。

a. Either Lee or Chy will display <u>his</u> collection. (單數代名詞)

b. Jan or Mary will bring <u>her</u> cassette player. (單數代名詞)

17. 兩個或兩個以上先行詞用 "and" 連接時，必須用複數代名詞。

a. The sotre sent Paula and Robin the kits that <u>they</u> had ordered.

b. The principal and teacher reached <u>their</u> decision.

18. 在完整句子和不完整句子中使用 then 和 as 時，句子中加入了代名詞，它們都是正確的句子，但在意義上卻有很大的不同。

a. My brother is taller than <u>I</u>. (不完全)

   My brother is taller than <u>I</u> am tall. (完全)

b. I understand Bill better than <u>she</u>. (不完全)

   I understand Bill better than <u>she</u> understands Bill. (完全)

c. I understand Bill better than <u>her</u>. (不完全)

   I understand Bill better than I understand <u>her</u>. (完全)

d. My brother played piano as often as <u>I</u>. (不完全且用主格)

My brother played piano as often as <u>I</u> played piano. (完全且用主格)

    e. He complained his brother as much (he complained) <u>us</u>.

(不完全且用受格)

He complained his brother as much as <u>we</u> (complained his brother).

(不完全且用主格)

19. 代名詞 there 的特殊問題

there 常被用做主詞,但它是虛主詞,因此常會被用錯。真正的主詞是在 there 之後,而在動詞之前。所以真正的主詞為單數時,動詞就用單數,真正的主詞為複數時,動詞就用複數。一般來說,there 可以和下列字連合使用。

    a. a 和 an

<u>There's</u> <u>a</u> letter for you from America.

<u>There'll</u> be <u>an</u> exhibition of Plcasso paintings in December.

    b. 沒有冠詞

<u>There</u> are ways in the jam.

    c. some, any 和 no

<u>There</u> are <u>some</u> changes in the printed programme.

Are <u>there</u> <u>any</u> lemons in the refrigerator?

<u>There</u> are <u>no</u> volunteers for a job like this!

    d. some, any 和 no 的複合字

Is <u>there</u> <u>anyone</u> here who can read Chinese?

<u>There</u> was <u>something</u> I wanted to show you.

<u>There</u> is <u>nothing</u> on my desk.

    e. 數字和數量的字

<u>There</u> are <u>eighteen</u> people coming to dinner.

<u>There</u> aren't <u>many</u> female students in that university.

<u>There'll</u> be <u>thousands</u> of fans in Chicago this Sunday.

    f. 明確的指定者,the, this, that 和 my 等字。

<u>There's</u> <u>the</u> fireplace.

There's <u>that</u> house.

There's <u>my</u> cat.

There's <u>this</u> car.

20. 代名詞 it 的特殊問題

   It 是另外一個常會用錯的代名詞，it 永遠放在句子中的第一個字，以便代替如下列較長的片語或子句。

   a. It is difficult to understand what he means. (It 代替 what he means 子句)

   b. It is said that the meeting will not be held.

      (It 代替 that the meeting will not be held 子句)

   c. It's no use worring. (It 代替 no use worring 片語)

21. It's 和 Its 意義完全不同，不可混淆。

   a. Who did it?　<u>It's</u> me. (It's=It was 或 It is；在文法上應是 It's I)

   b. This dog is so tiny.　Its tail is very short. (Its 為代名詞，it 的所有格)

22. there 和 their 不要混淆，雖然發音相同，但是它們的意義完全不同。there 可以當副詞，名詞和驚嘆詞。their 則為代名詞 they 的所有格。

   a. I was very pleased with the Wilsons for thinking of me when they decided to expand <u>their</u> company. (their 為所有格代名詞)

   b. They sat <u>there</u> in the stands while I got hot dogs. (there 為副詞)

   c. They each performed to the best of <u>their</u> ability. (their 所有格代名詞)

   d. <u>There</u> are a lot of books in Congress Library. (There 為虛主詞)

23. One 這個代名詞的複雜問題，one 為單數，ones 為複數，one's 為所有格，而 oneself 則為反身代名詞。

   a. Do you have a house?

      Yes, I have <u>one</u>.

   b. There are three books on the table; an English <u>one</u> and two Chinese <u>ones</u>.

   c. One must keep <u>one's</u> promise.

　　　d. One must respect <u>oneself</u>.

24. No one 與 None 有相同的，也有不同的。no one 是指人，而 None 可用在人或事物。

　　　a. <u>No one</u> is right forever.

　　　b. Is there anybody at classroom?

　　　　No, there is <u>none</u>.

　　　c. Do you have any money to buy a radio?

　　　　No, I have <u>none</u>.

25. This 是單數，these 為複數，而 that 為單數，those 則為複數。它們可以為代名詞，也可以做形容詞。

　　　a. <u>This</u> cup is in front of us. (This 為形容詞)

　　　b. <u>That</u> spoon is on the other side of the table. (That 為形容詞)

　　　c. <u>This</u> is a crystal vase. (This 為代名詞)

　　　d. <u>That</u> is my father's van. (That 為代名詞)

　　　e. <u>These</u> apples are very good. (These 為形容詞)

　　　f. <u>Those</u> automobiles belong to my uncle. (Those 為形容詞)

　　　g. Don't look at <u>these</u>. (these 為代名詞)

　　　h. <u>Those</u> who don't wish to go need not do so. (Those 為代名詞)

第六章 ｜ 形容詞（Adjectives）

1. 形容詞是修飾名詞和代名詞的字，它們也可以修飾動名詞。如此一來，一個句子或一篇文章，唸起來較優美，也比較有感情，不會讓人感到枯燥無味。

2. 形容詞通常放在它們所修飾的名詞和代名詞之前，但有時會放在句中或句尾，不過非常少見。無論如何，距離不能太遠，否則會造成困擾，產生不明不白的狀況。

   a. We stayed at the Grand Canyon for <u>several</u> days.

   b. Silver Spring is a <u>famous</u> city in Maryland.

   c. Soon I went indoors and fell into a <u>deep</u> sleep.

   d. Our first lady is an <u>intelligent</u> lady.

   e. The campus <u>large</u> and <u>beautiful</u>, astonished us. (較正確)

   The campus astonished us, <u>large and beautiful</u>. (不太好距離太遠)

   f. The dog is <u>gentle</u>.

   g. The tent, <u>warm</u> and <u>dry</u>, was under the tree.

   h. The <u>spicy</u> smell of <u>warm</u> apples filled the air.

   i. I was <u>sleepy</u>, and I longed for my <u>comfortable</u> bed.

3. 一個句子裡如果有兩個以上的形容詞時，它們的順序歸納出來有兩個大原則。

   A. 短字應放在長字之前面

   a. My bed is <u>light</u> and <u>beautiful</u>.

   b. Her nightgown is <u>red</u> and <u>fashionable</u>.

   c. I watched until the sky was <u>bright</u> with <u>twinkling</u> stars.

   d. Our teacher is <u>young</u> and <u>handsome</u>.

B. 冠詞（或代名詞當形容詞用）→大小→年代→顏色→現在分詞或
過去分詞當形容詞用→專有名詞當形容詞用→名詞當形容詞用→
名詞。

  a. <u>The</u> <u>huge</u>, <u>ancient</u>, <u>black</u>, and <u>white</u>, <u>Egyptian</u> picture was diplayed
our museum last month. (很多形容詞它是修飾名詞 picture)

  b. <u>Some</u> <u>short</u>, <u>brown</u>, and <u>active</u> rabbits ran around my back yard all the
time. (很多形容詞只修飾名詞 rabbits)

  c. <u>There</u> are <u>a lot of</u> <u>straight</u> high ways in America. (很多形容詞只修飾
名詞 high ways)

4. 普通形容詞

這個字的本身就是形容詞，不做其它用途，往往表示狀態或性質之
類。

  a. A <u>bright</u> moon rode down the <u>western</u> sky.

  b. It shed a <u>pale</u> light on the <u>quiet</u> countryside.

  c. <u>Long</u> meadows spread out to <u>two</u> hills in the distance.

  d. The smell of the <u>wild</u> grass was <u>strong</u>.

  e. The <u>only</u> sound was the <u>sharp</u> crackle of the fire.

  f. I was <u>sad</u> and <u>happy</u> at the <u>same</u> time.

  g. An <u>old</u> dog lay in the middle of the <u>weedy</u> garden.

5. 專有名詞當形容詞

專有名詞當形容詞用，不過仍然要用大寫。

  a. The quartet sang several <u>Irish</u> songs.

  b. The gold watch was made by <u>Swiss</u> watchmaker.

  c. She is a fine <u>Spanish</u> dancer.

  d. Many <u>Australian</u> people are of <u>British</u> origin.

  e. The <u>Egyptian</u> mummies are on display on the first floor.

  f. The movie is based on a popular <u>Russian</u> novel.

  g. In <u>Canadian</u> football there are twelve players on a team.

  h. The <u>Indian</u> weaver made a blanket on a wooden loom.

i. The movie is based on a popular <u>Chinese</u> novel.

6. 名詞當形容詞

普通名詞當做形容詞去修飾另一個名詞，主要是找不到適合的形容詞，不得已將名詞做為形容詞用。但要注意的是，將比較不重要的名詞做為形容詞去修飾另一個比較重要的名詞。

   a. In general, Americans have a lot of <u>credit</u> cards.

   b. Would you like to drink some <u>orange</u> juice.

   c. How many <u>spring</u> jackets and <u>winter</u> jackets do you have?

   d. Did you enjoy his <u>birthday</u> party last night?

   e. Tell me!　Which one is better between <u>brick</u> wall and wooden wall?

   f. I always bring my <u>grocery</u> list on weekend.

7. 複合形容詞

將數個名詞用連字號或不用連字號連在一起當做形容詞用。

   a. Mr. Lee is a <u>well-known</u> prfoessor at Maryland University.

   b. A <u>hit-and-run</u> driver is a serious criminal.

   c. <u>Crossword</u> puzzle is very interesting.

   d. Don't forget your past-due bill.

8. 代名詞當形容詞

一般來說，很多代名詞兼負著代名詞與形容詞的功能。

A. 人稱代名詞所有格當形容詞

   a. He and his brother strenuously object to <u>my</u> smoking.

   b. They each performed to the best of <u>their</u> ability.

   c. All of the members brought <u>their</u> wives.

B. 指示代名詞當形容詞。

   a. <u>This</u> book is mine and that book is yours.

   b. Please put <u>these</u> flowers on the living room table.

   c. Do you know <u>those</u> people in the room?

C. 疑問代名詞當形容詞

   a. <u>Whose</u> umbrella is left here?

      b. <u>Which</u> movies do you like the best?

      c. <u>What</u> kind of salad does your girl friend prefer?

   D.　不定代名詞當形容詞

      a. <u>Each</u> rose costs 100 (one hundred) dollars.

      b. <u>Several</u> people stayed at train station about ten minutes ago.

      c. I bought <u>some</u> fruits at organic super market yesterday.

9.　數量形容詞

   用來表示數目或數量的形容詞。

      a. I have <u>many</u> books.

      b. Don't pour too <u>much</u> water into the flowers.

      c. Do you have <u>any</u> money to lend me?

      d. Don't worry!　He has <u>enough</u> time to catch the train.

      e. I just ate <u>two</u> slices of bread about an hour ago.

      f. He was the <u>fifty-second</u> (52nd) President of the United States.

      g. About <u>half</u> students went out the classroom.

      h. There were <u>one-third</u> (1/3) watermelons stolen.

10.　補語形容詞

   通常在連繫動詞之後，一方面當做主詞的補語，一方面又有修飾主詞的功能。

      a. After a long trip, everybody was <u>tire</u> and <u>thirsty</u>.

      b. This stadium was <u>crowded</u> and <u>noisy</u>.

      c. John became <u>angry</u>, because Jen was taking away his pen.

      d. Mrs. Taylor looks <u>happy</u> after she went to vacation.

      e. The astronaut, <u>floating</u> in space, repaired the satellite.

      f. <u>Repaired</u> by the astronaut, the satellite again sent data back to the earth.

11.　現在分詞和過去分詞當形容詞

   在它們的意義上有相當的差異，現在分詞有主動的意思，而過去分詞則有被動的意味。

a. That story is very <u>interesting</u>.

b. I'm <u>interested</u> in his long speech about Chinese history.

c. It's dangerous to bother the <u>sleeping</u> dog.

d. He looked so <u>slept</u> because he went to bed too late.

e. I'm <u>excited</u> by this story.

f. She was never <u>bored</u> with my talking.

g. The movie star was quite <u>enchanting</u> to be with.

h. He is a most <u>interesting</u> man.

i. The old tin mine was quite <u>exhausted</u>.

j. All doors were <u>locked</u> we couldn't go into the house.

12. 形容詞的形成

很多英文字天生就是形容詞的性質，不需要做任何的變化。但也有很多形容詞是由名詞，動詞甚至由形容詞變化而來。

如 ： health-----healthy, anger-----angry, cloud-----cloudy, day-----daily, harm-----harmful, wonder-----wonderful, value-----valueless, honor-----honorable, comfort-----comfortable, form-----formal, nature-----natural, temper-----temperate, base-----basic, practice-----practical, self-----selfish, fame-----famous, pride-----proud, please-----pleasant, favor-----favorite, suit-----suitable, act-----active, talk-----talkative, trouble-----troublesome, formal-----informal, honest-----dishonest, direct-----indirect, known-----unknown, wise-----unwise, like-----unlike, etc.

13. 形容詞的比較

A. 初級———一個東西無從比較時用。

a. The canned goods make my backpack <u>heavy</u>.

b. This basketball player is very <u>tall</u>.

c. We need read many <u>good</u> books.

d. A <u>famous</u> French museum is called Louvre.

B. 比較級———二個東西比較時用。

a. My brother is <u>taller</u> than I.

b. This table is <u>heavier</u> than that chair.

c. He felt a little <u>better</u> today.

d. The <u>shorter</u> twin is the captain of the squard.

C. 最高級──三個或三個以上東西比較時用。

a. He is <u>the most reliable</u> person in that group.

b. New York is <u>the largest</u> city in U.S.A.

c. Some of <u>the most valuable</u> objects require special temperature and humidity control.

d. This is <u>the darkest</u> of the five copies.

14. 形容詞比較的一般規則

A. 形容詞為一個音節或兩個音節時，原級加 er 成為比較級，加 est 成為最高級。

原級	比較級	最高級
funny	funnier	the funniest
dull	duller	the dullest
blue	bluer	the bluest
old	older	the oldest
clever	cleverer	the cleverest
sad	sadder	the saddest
fancy	fancier	the fanciest
lonely	lonelier	the loneliest

B. 形容詞為三個或三個以上音節時，原級加上 more 或 less 成為比較級，加 the most 或 the least 成為最高級。

原級	比較級	最高級
terrible	more terrible	the most terrible
impossible	more impossible	the most impossible
ambitious	less ambitious	the least ambitious
difficult	more difficult	the most difficult

C. 不規則變化的形容詞

原級	比較級	最高級
good	better	the best
many	more	the most
much	more	the most
little	less	the least
bad	worse	the worst

D. 有些形容詞加 er 或 est 之後，唸起來感覺上有點怪怪的，最好加上 more 成為比較級，加上 the most 成為最高級。

原級	比較級	最高級
charming	more charming	the most charming
famous	more famous	the most famous
obese	more obese	the most obese
moving	more moving	the most moving
pleasing	more pleasing	the most pleasing
vicious	more vicious	the most vicious

15. 使用形容詞比較時不可雙重比較

    a. Your party ended <u>sooner</u> than I would have liked. (正確)

       Your party ended <u>more sooner</u> than I would have liked. (錯誤)

    b. That was <u>the funniest</u> joke we ever heard. (正確)

       That was <u>the most funniest</u> joke we ever heard. (錯誤)

16. 使用形容詞比較時，必須要很清楚，整個句子要明確，說明什麼東西在比較。

    a. The average temperature in Dallas is <u>higher than</u> New York. (不清楚)

       The average temperature in Dallas is <u>higher than that</u> in New York. (清楚)

    b. The hide of the rhinoceros is <u>harder than</u> the alligator. (不清楚)

The hide of the rhinoceros is <u>harder than that</u> of the alligator. (清楚)

17. 使用形容詞比較級時，不可將自己包括在內，以免造成不合理狀態。

  a. John's hair is <u>longer than any</u> in the classroom. (不合理)

   John's hair is <u>longer than any other</u> in the classroom. (合理)

  b. Mary is <u>more beautiful than anybody</u> in the school. (不合理)

   Mary is <u>more beautiful than anybody else</u> in the school. (合理)

  c. Our school is <u>larger than any</u> in the city. (不合理)

   Our school is <u>larger than any other</u> in the city. (合理)

  d. Jan is <u>funnier than anybody</u> in her class. (不合理)

   Jan is <u>funnier than anybody else</u> in her class. (合理)

18. 定冠詞 the 加上形容詞表示整個族群，動詞要用複數，千萬不可以 a 或 an 來代替 the。

  a. You can always judge a society by the way <u>the old are</u> cared for. (正確)

   You can always judge a society by the way <u>an old is</u> cared for. (錯誤)

  b. <u>The poor are</u> thousands in the U.S.A. (正確)

   <u>A poor is</u> thousands in the U.S.A. (錯誤)

19. 不可使用形容詞本身當做個體，如果要表明個體時，必須使用形容詞加上名詞。

  a. He is an old. (錯誤)

   He is an old man. (正確)

  b. He is a young with a lot of ambition. (錯誤)

   He is a young man with a lot of ambition. (正確)

20. 有些形容詞也可被修飾成代表整體，動詞則用複數。

  a. <u>The extremely poor</u> are also thousands in Mainland China.

  b. <u>The super rich</u> are a lot in Japan.

21. 有時候一些 the 加形容詞之前有 both (and), either (or), neither (nor)等等，這時候 the 可以省略掉。

  a. Both (the) young and (the) old enjoyed themselves at the party.

b. Either (the) rich or (the) poor can't stand rigid winter.

22. 整體關係可以為一般的或抽象的形容詞，如：the unknown, the supernatural, the unexpected 等等，它們的動詞是單數。

    a. <u>The unknown</u> is always something to be feared.

    b. <u>The unexpected happens</u> anywhere and anytime.

23. 使用形容詞比較時，不可將不同性質，毫無關聯的東西互相比較。

    a. This <u>building</u> is larger than this <u>yard</u>. (錯誤)

    This <u>building</u> is larger than that <u>building</u>. (正確)

    b. <u>Iron</u> is heavier than <u>cotton</u>. (錯誤)

    This <u>iron</u> is heavier than that <u>iron</u>. (正確)

    This <u>cotton</u> is heavier than that <u>cotton</u>. (正確)

24. 有些形容詞本身已經是百分之百的完美，因此不可以再做比較。

    a. Yesterday's car accident was <u>fatal</u>. (正確)

    Yesterday's car accident was <u>more fatal</u>. (錯誤)

    b. Your report is <u>perfect</u>. (正確)

    Your report is <u>more perfect</u>. (錯誤)

    c. Our National Museum collected a <u>unique</u> picture in the world. (正確)

    Our National Museum collected a <u>more unique</u> picture in the world. (錯誤)

25. 有些形容詞具有雙重身分，既可以當形容詞又可當副詞，但是它們所修飾的字仍然不同。形容詞身分時修飾名詞，副詞身分時修飾動詞或副詞。

    a. The next train will be <u>less</u> crowded than this one. (副詞)

    b. It happened just when we <u>least</u> expected it. (副詞)

    c. If you don't want to get fat, eat <u>less</u> food. (形容詞)

    d. You haven't the <u>least</u> chance of success. (形容詞)

26. 限定形容詞子句是認定它所修飾的名詞而非限定形容詞子句則不認定它所修飾的名詞。因此，在非限定子句中，不可省略關係代名詞，也不可使用關係代名詞 that。而在限定的子句中不可使用標點符號 ","

將它與主要子句分開。

　　a. A student <u>who (or that) studies hard always</u> gets a good grade. (限定子句)

　　b. He has already finished the painting <u>which (or that) the landlord asked</u>. (限定子句)

　　c. He has two sons, <u>who work in the post office</u>. (非限定子句)

　　d. English grammar, <u>which I like very much</u>, is good for me. (非限定子句)

27. 最高級形容詞也可以修飾複數名詞。

　　a. My friend is <u>very tall</u>.

　　　My friend is <u>much taller</u> than I.

　　　My friend is <u>much the tallest</u> of all our team.

　　b. This building is <u>very high</u>.

　　　This building is <u>much higher</u> than that building over there.

　　　This building is <u>much the highest</u> of all this area.

28. 形容詞同等級的比較

　A. 肯定句的比較

　　a. He is <u>as</u> old <u>as</u> his wife (is).

　　b. I am <u>as</u> happy <u>as</u> my wife is.

　　c. Today's weather was <u>as</u> humid <u>as</u> yesterday's was.

　B. 否定句的比較

　　a. My older brother is <u>not so</u> short <u>as</u> I am.

　　b. This wall is <u>not so</u> hard <u>as</u> it looks.

　　c. The temperature <u>isn't so</u> low <u>as</u> (it was) last Sunday.

第七章 │ 連接詞（Conjunctions）

1. 連接詞是連接字，片語，子句或句子之用。

2. 對等連接詞

   連接相等的詞類，片語，子句或句子。

   如：and, but, for, so, therefore, still & however 等等。

   A. 連接名詞或代名詞

      a. The mom <u>and</u> her three kids went to market this morning.

      b. Would you like coffee <u>or</u> tea?

      c. He is poor <u>but</u> frugal.

      d. She <u>and</u> he are the same age.

      e. It can't be done by you <u>nor</u> me <u>nor</u> anyone.

   B. 連接動詞

      a. The car swerved <u>and</u> ran off the road.

      b. We tried <u>but</u> failed.

      c. You may copy <u>or</u> write this article.

   C. 連接副詞

      a. You should drink soup slowly <u>and</u> carefully.

      b. He jumped highly <u>but</u> hurtly.

      c. She talked the car accident orderly <u>or</u> thoroughly.

   D. 連接形容詞

      a. This street is narrow <u>and</u> long.

      b. My new car is beautiful <u>but</u> expensive.

      c. Her grand mother is old <u>and</u> skinny.

   E. 連接獨立句或附屬子句

a. Have a good time, <u>but</u> don't stay out too late.

b. We ran on the beach, <u>for</u> the water was too cold.

c. The play is long, <u>yet</u> is held my interest to the end.

d. The coach blew the whistle, <u>and</u> the runners began the race.

e. You rake the leaves, <u>and</u> I will sweep the path.

f. Did Nancy finish her report, <u>or</u> is she still working on it?

  F.　連接不定詞

a. He started to shout <u>and</u> sing.

b. She began to cry <u>and</u> tear.

3.　相關連接詞

連接相關的詞類，片語，子句或句子。但是它們卻相相對對的同時使用。

如：both-----and, either-----or, neither-----nor, not only-----but also

和 whether-----or 等等。

  A.　連接名詞或代名詞

a. <u>Both</u> John <u>and</u> Harry are teachers.

b. <u>Either</u> he <u>or</u> you have to cook dinner.

c. It is hard to say <u>whether</u> blue <u>or</u> red it the better color.

d. Roller-skating is <u>not only</u> ease <u>but also</u> fun.

e. Show your pass to <u>both</u> the hall monitor <u>and</u> the principal.

  B.　連接動詞

a. <u>Either</u> type the report <u>or</u> write it neatly.

b. I <u>neither</u> drank, <u>nor</u> smoked.

c. Our club members will <u>either</u> make the decorations <u>or</u> bring refreshments.

  C.　連接副詞

a. Frank finished his homework <u>not only</u> quickly <u>but also</u> correctly.

b. Mary cooked <u>both</u> creatively <u>and</u> skillfully.

  D.　連接形容詞

    a. Maryland's winter is <u>not only</u> cold <u>but also</u> snowy.

    b. Our neighbor's dog is <u>neither</u> tall <u>nor</u> short.

E.　連接介詞片語

    a. Can you put my hand phone <u>either</u> on the book table <u>or</u> beside the flower vase?

    b. He drove <u>neither</u> to the left <u>nor</u> to the right.

F.　連接子句或句子

    a. <u>Either</u> we buy it now, <u>or</u> we will wait for the next sale.

    b. <u>Not only</u> is he a good basketball player, <u>but</u> he is <u>also</u> a fine football athlete. (注意倒裝句)

4.　從屬連接詞

將主要子句與附屬子句連接起來的字，一般來說附屬子句多半為副詞子句的意味。

如：because, if, before, since, when, whenever, unless, until, etc.

    a. We played chess <u>while</u> we waited for the rain to stop.

    b. <u>Although</u> both teams played their best, only one could be the winner.

    c. Jan stood <u>where</u> she could see the finish of the race.

    d. <u>Whenever</u> the cat climbs that evergreen tree, the birds chase it away.

    e. <u>Before</u> the sun rose, we left for the beach.

5.　相關附屬連接詞

這種連接詞不但成雙成對，而且最重要的是連接子句之間的成因與結果。

如：so-----that, such-----that, such a-----that, so-----a-----that, etc.

    a. She got up <u>so</u> late <u>that</u> she missed her subway.

    b. It is <u>such</u> nice weather <u>that</u> I would like to go to the beach.

    c. She is <u>such a</u> kindly woman <u>that</u> we love her.

    d. It was <u>so</u> lovely <u>a</u> day <u>that</u> we went to picnic.

6.　片語連接詞

顧名思義這些連接詞不是單字而是片語，片語擔任連接詞的角色。

如：as long as, in case, as soon as, as if, etc.

    a. Mr. Lee and I have been friends <u>as long as</u> we have known each other.

    b. <u>As soon as</u> I get news, I'll tell you.

    c. <u>In case</u> it'll rain, we can't go to picnic.

7. 副詞連接詞

原來是副詞，但它們卻能將獨立的句子連接起來，使整個句子的意義更加完整。

如：accordingly, besides, however, otherwise, after all, at the same time, on the other hand, etc.

要注意的是，這些連接詞往往擺在兩個句子的中間，而且前後要用點號 "，" 分開。

    a. Our manager is trustful, <u>in addition</u>, he is very kind.

    b. He had cried for twenty minutes, <u>finally</u>, his mom came to hug him.

    c. We met a car accident, <u>therefore</u>, we lost to enjoy our sister's birthday party.

8. Not only-----but also 和 neither-----nor 兩組連接詞在使用時，如果將 Not only 或 Neither 放在句首或否定句時，要用倒裝句，即動詞放在主詞前面。此外，but also 連在一起用時，also 可以省略，分開用時不可省略。

    a. Not only was he a singer, <u>but (also)</u> he was a dancer.

      = <u>Not only</u> was he a singer, <u>but</u> he <u>also</u> was a dancer.

    b. <u>Neither</u> John <u>nor</u> Betty is at home.

    c. Bob can't go, and <u>neither</u> can I.

9. 連接詞 so 在口語中常常被過度使用，在寫作時要盡可能少用。

    a. I have finished writing my first draft, <u>so</u> I am ready to revise it. (非正式)

      <u>Since</u> I have finished writing my first draft, I am ready to revise it. (正式)

    b. He went early <u>so</u> he might get a good seat. (非正式)

He went early <u>so that</u> he might get a good seat. (正式)

10. 有些連接詞與介詞同字，但是它們的功能卻不相同。連接詞是可以連接子句，而介詞只能連接名詞而已。

    a. I haven't seen him <u>since</u> this morning. (介詞)

    I haven't seen him <u>since</u> he left this morning. (連接詞)

    b. I will come <u>after</u> supper. (介詞)

    <u>After</u> he goes, we shall eat. (連接詞)

    c. Who will act <u>as</u> teacher? (介詞)

    He does not speak <u>as</u> the other people do. (連接詞)

    d. We plant some flowers <u>before</u> our house. (介詞)

    I will do it now <u>before</u> I forget it. (連接詞)

11. 有些連接詞可以接沒有 "to" 的不定詞。

    a. I've done everything you wanted <u>but</u> make the beds.

    b. I'd rather stay at home <u>than</u> go for a walk.

12. 連接詞 however, even so, therefore, consequently, nonetheless nevertheless, etc.這些連接詞將兩個句子連接成一個句子時，在它們的前面用分號 ";" 在它們的後面用點號 ","。

    a. Everyone attended the meeting; <u>however</u>, we could not make a decision.

    b. He was the only candidate; <u>therefore</u>, he was slected.

    c. He is the popular candidate; <u>consequently</u>, he will be elected.

    d. We are going; <u>nevertheless</u>, we shall return.

    e. She was very tired; <u>nonetheless</u>, she kept on working.

    f. It's raining; even so, we have to go out.

13. 連接詞 however, even so, therefore, consequently, nonetheless, nevertheless, etc.這些連接詞不將兩個句子連接，而是放在新句子的句首，以便完成整個意義的說明時，在它們之後要加個點號 ","。

    a. Everyone attended the meeting.   <u>However</u>, we could not make a decision.

b. He was the only candidate. <u>Therefore</u>, he was elected.

14. And, but, yet, so, thus, hence, etc.這些連接詞將兩個句子連接成一個句子時，在它們的前面要加點號 "," 。

    a. He did the work, <u>and</u> he did it well.

    b. I was very angry, <u>but</u> I didn't say anything.

    c. He is poor, <u>yet</u> he is honest.

    d. As the lion is king of beasts, <u>so</u> is the eagle king of the birds.

    e. He studied hard, <u>thus</u> he got high marks.

    f. It is very late, <u>hence</u> you must go to bed.

15. And, but, yet, so, thus, hence, etc.這些連接詞不將兩個句子連接，而是放在新句子之句首時，它們的後面要加點號 "," 。

    a. Most people disagreed his plan.

    <u>Thus</u>, we decides that he was wrong.

    b. The government does not wish to raise taxes.

    <u>Hence</u>, it cannot give more money to the schools.

16. Although, even though, though, in spite of the fact, despite the fact that, because, since, as, in order that, so that, etc.這些連接詞在介紹一個句子的第一部分時，需加點號 "," 以便區隔句子的另外一部分。

    a. <u>Although</u> my house is small, it is very comfortable.

    b. <u>Though</u> I fail, I shall try again.

    c. <u>In spite of the fact that</u> it was raining, I went to supermaket.

17. Although, even though, though, in spite of the fact, despite the fact that, because, since, as, in order that, so that, etc.這些連接詞如果是介紹句子的第二部分時，不要使用點號 "," 。

    a. My house is very comfortable <u>although</u> it is very small.

    b. I went to supermarket <u>in spite of the fact that</u> it was raining.

    c. I shall try again <u>though</u> I fail.

第八章 │ **感嘆詞** (Interjection)

1. 感嘆詞是對於喜悅，哀怨，稱讚，意外，驚恐，問候等等的事情，表現很強烈的感情，而發出很不尋常的聲音。

   a. <u>Aha!</u>　I know you were hiding there.

   b. <u>Oops!</u>　I punched in the wrong numbers.

   c. <u>Ouch!</u>　The water is still very hot.

   d. <u>Oh! Boy!</u>　I found your store finally.

   e. <u>My Goodness!</u>　He lost his watch.

   f. <u>Damn it!</u>　The thief stole my jacket.

   g. <u>Look!</u>　There is a beautiful bird!

   h. <u>Hallo!</u>　Good morning!

2. 感嘆詞與句子的其它部分，沒有任何文法上的問題。不過感嘆詞之後的句子，它的第一個字的字首要大寫。

   a. <u>Ugh!</u>　There's a skunk somewhere!

   b. <u>Wonderful!</u>　We can go!

   c. <u>Hey!</u>　Be careful of that fire!

   d. <u>Aw!</u>　It wasn't anything.

   e. <u>Well!</u>　I quess that's that.

3. 古今中外，我們人類對於事情好壞的驚嘆，所發出的聲音都大同小異，只不過訴諸文字則有所不同而已。

   a. <u>Oh!</u>　You surprised me!

   b. <u>Wow!</u>　Am I tired!

   c. <u>Well!</u>　I did my best.

   d. <u>Well!</u>　I'm just not sure.

第九章 | **動詞** (Verbs)

1. 在英語文裡，一個句子除了主詞之外，最重要的是動詞，這兩個詞加起來就可以成為完整的句子。主詞的一舉一動要靠動詞來表示，而主詞的各種狀態，也要靠動詞來完成，因此動詞顯得異常的重要且複雜。

2. 動作動詞

   大部分的動詞均為動作動詞，它們均表示主詞的動作，不管是身體的或精神上的。

   A. 可以看得見的動作。

   　a. I <u>used</u> a computer in math class.

   　b. I <u>jogged</u> a mile today.

   　c. They <u>make</u> unusual pottery.

   　d. The Indians <u>paint</u> designs on the pottery.

   　e. The Maricopa Indians <u>teach</u> their children this craft.

   B. 看不見的動作

   　a. Todd <u>understands</u> the science assignment.

   　b. They <u>need</u> two kinds of clay for this pottery.

   　c. Often members of my family sit silently and <u>listen</u> for these noises of the house.

   　d. Even good friends sometimes <u>disagree</u>.

   　e. April <u>auditioned</u> for the lead role.

3. 及物動詞

   動作涉及到人或事物，因此有受詞，同時可以有被動語態。

   　a. He <u>writes</u> <u>a letter</u> for his friend.

b. They sometimes <u>use a toothpick</u>.

c. One kind <u>forms a vessel</u>.

d. His wife <u>cooks three meals</u> for his family every day.

4. 不及物動詞

動作不涉及到人或事物，因此沒有受詞，同時不能變成被動語態。

a. My brother <u>exercises</u> in the morning every day.

b. He <u>jumps</u> very high.

c. Your baby <u>smiles</u> all the time.

d. The sun <u>rises</u> at 7 o'clock in summer.

5. 連繫動詞

雖然本身沒有任何動作，但它們可以將主詞和其它名詞，形容詞，或介詞片語等等連接起來，最後完成完整的句子。但要注意的是不可連接副詞，除了 be 動詞之外，還有 become, appear, feel, look, remain, seem, smell, sound, taste, etc.

a. They <u>have been</u> happier.

b. Juliet <u>looked</u> scary in her costume.

c. Wilson <u>scounded</u> happy about the new job.

d. Bill <u>feels</u> uncertain about the race.

6. 連繫動詞有時也可以為動作動詞，要如何區分，可將 be 動詞代替之後，看看意義是否合理，如果合理就是連繫動詞，如果不合理就是動作動詞。

a. The vinegar <u>tasted</u> sour.

The vinegar is sour.

(意義上合理，故 tasted 是連繫動詞)

b. I <u>tasted</u> the soup.

I am the soup.

(意義上不合理，故 tasted 是動作動詞)

c. He <u>became</u> sad after he heard the news.

He was sad after he heard the news.

（意義上合理，故 became 是連繫動詞）

7. 助動詞

往往把助動詞擺在主動詞之前，輔助主動詞完成動作的一切情況。除
了 be 動詞之外，還有 do, does, did, can, could, has, had, shall, should,
will, would, etc.

8. 助動詞 can, do, shall, will 的用法

   A. 現在式

      a. She <u>can</u> solve the problem easily.

      b. <u>Do</u> you feel cold?

      c. I <u>shall</u> be a teacher next year.

      d. It <u>will</u> be a nice day tomorrow.

   B. 過去式

      a. I <u>could</u> sing when I was young.

      b. <u>Did</u> you call me last night?

      c. I thought I <u>should</u> succeed.

      d. They said it <u>would</u> be fine.

9. 助動詞 dare 和 need 的用法

   A. 現在式

      a. He <u>dare</u> not jump from the top of that wall.

      b. <u>Need</u> you go so soon?

   B. 過去式

      a. The explorer <u>dared</u> the dangers of the icy north. (主動詞)

      b. He <u>dared</u> say. (助動詞)

      c. We <u>needed</u> a computer very much. (主動詞)

10. 助動詞 could, may, might, must, ought to, should 的用法

   A. 現在式

      a. I <u>could</u> come tomorrow.

      b. <u>May</u> we go home now?

      c. We went abroad that we <u>might</u> learn something of the culture of other countries.

d. She <u>must</u> be a very good dancer.

e. Prices <u>ought to</u> come down this spring.

f. You <u>should</u> try to fix that chair again.

B. must, ought to and should 的過去式均為 had to

a. He <u>had to</u> study very hard for his entrance examination last year.

b. You <u>had to</u> come to the meeting yesterday.

11. Must have, ought to have 加上過去分詞，表示過去發生的事情有很強烈的可能性。

a. They <u>must have gone</u> to bed because all the lights in the house are out.

b. By the looks of the street, it <u>must have rained</u> while we were in the movie theater.

c. You <u>must have worked</u> very fast in order to have finished that work so quickly.

d. You <u>ought to have told</u> him about that.

e. They <u>ought not to have sent</u> her a present.

12. May have, might have, could have, should have 加上過去分詞，表示過去的事情，很有可能發生。

a. They <u>may have gone</u> home already, because I don't see them here.

b. I haven't any idea where Sue is, but she <u>might have gone</u> to the movie with John.

c. One of the strangers <u>may have stolen</u> the money.

d. She <u>could have ridden</u> in the car with us.

e. She <u>could have shopped</u> by phone.

f. She <u>should have helped</u> me clean the typewriter.

g. He <u>shouldn't have drunk</u> wine with his lunch.

13. Be able to 加原型動詞是描述某人的能力。

A. 現在式

a. He <u>is able to</u> speak English, Spanish, and French.

b. He <u>is able to</u> play piano.

B. 過去式

a. He <u>was able to</u> come yesterday.

b. He <u>could ride</u> the bicycle very well.

c. I <u>could have climbed</u> that tree when I was young.

C. 未來式

a. I <u>shall be able to</u> come tomorrow.

b. <u>Will he be able</u> to get that?

14. Do, does, did 在句子中有時候是加強表達的語氣，不可與助動詞的功能相混淆。

a. I agree your idea. (一般)

I <u>do</u> agree your idea. (加強)

b. <u>Do</u> you have any sugar? (一般)

Yes, I <u>do</u> have. (加強)

c. <u>Did</u> you forget to mail my book? (一般)

Yes, I <u>did</u> forget.　Please forgive me. (加強)

15. Don't 和 doesn't 必須與它們的主詞一致。

a. Jan <u>doesn't</u> exercise enough in winter.

b. Those answers <u>don't</u> make sense.

16. 不定詞

由動詞演變而來，也就是動詞原型前加 to，不是真正的動詞卻仍然有動詞的意味。

A. 當名詞用

a. <u>To try</u> is everybody's hope. (主格)

b. <u>To wait</u> for the doctor seems boring. (主格)

c. <u>To jog</u> a mile every morning is my hobby. (主格)

d. I like <u>to read</u> different books. (受格)

e. A lot of people do not like <u>to travel</u> by sea. (受格)

f. She tried <u>to pass</u> the TOEFL examination. (受格)

g. They promised <u>to return</u> soon. (受格)

B. 當主格補語用

a. My hobby is <u>to travel</u>.

b. In this summer, all I want to do is <u>to arrange</u> my back yard.

c. My ambition is <u>to become</u> a good teacher.

C. 當同位語用

a. His goal, <u>to jog</u>, only lasted a few weeks.

b. Our plan, <u>to finish the final report</u>, was approved by the profesor.

D. 當形容詞用

a. You may ask your mother's decision <u>to see the movie</u>.

b. He bought a new shoes <u>to wear for the raining day</u>.

c. The place <u>to meet</u> is the public library.

E. 當副詞用

a. <u>To protect yourself</u>, you need to seal the belt.

b. We all live <u>to eat</u>.

c. This math problem is hard <u>to slove</u>.

F. 當虛詞 it 的同位語用

a. It always closes the door <u>to leave the home</u>.

b. It is worthy <u>to serve your customers</u>.

17. 不定詞的 to 和介詞的 to 不可混淆。

a. You need <u>to</u> alter the length of the skirt. (不定詞)

b. The coarse salt can be used <u>to</u> help melt snow on the roadways. (不定詞)

c. They go <u>to</u> school at 8 o'clock. (介詞)

d. Please pass this pen <u>to</u> him. (介詞)

18. 沒有 to 的不定詞用法

A. 在感官動詞之後，需指出第二個動作動詞時，如：feel, hear, listen to, look at, notice, see, watch, etc.

a. None one <u>saw</u> him <u>leave</u>.

b. I like to <u>hear</u> her <u>sing</u>.

B. 在使役動詞之後，需指出第二個動作動詞時，如：bid, have, let, make, etc.

    a. Don't <u>let</u> him <u>come</u>.

    b. The teacher <u>made</u> Sue <u>work</u> hard.

C. 在下列字或片語之後時，如：but, except, cannot but, do nothing but, etc.

    a. She never does anything <u>except</u> <u>complain</u>.

    b. He does nothing <u>but</u> <u>play</u> all day.

D. 在 help 這個動詞之後，可有可無 to.

    a. He <u>helped</u> me <u>move</u> the heavy table.

    b. He <u>helped</u> me to <u>move</u> the heavy table.

E. 當我們希望有些動作需要執行，不是靠自己，而是在我們教唆之下，要求別人去完成而使用 have 或 get 再加上主動詞的過去分詞。

    a. I <u>have</u> my hair <u>cut</u> once a month.

    b. she is going to <u>have</u> her nails <u>manicured</u>.

    c. Let's <u>get</u> our car <u>fixed</u> first.

19. 不可隨便使用其它詞類將不定詞分開，外觀上看起來不像不定詞之外，在文法上也不太合理。

    a. My mom asked me <u>to</u> immediately <u>come</u> home. (不合理)

       My mom asked me <u>to come</u> home immediately. (合理)

    b. He promised <u>to</u> carefully <u>drive</u> the new car. (不合理)

       He promised <u>to drive</u> the new car carefully. (合理)

    c. Our teacher planed <u>to</u> quickly <u>write</u> his second book. (不合理)

       Our teacher planed <u>to write</u> his second book quickly. (合理)

20. 不定詞如果接某些動詞時，為了避免重複，可以將不定詞的原式省略，不僅僅用 to.

    a. I don't know that bad guy, and I don't <u>want to</u> (know that bad guy).

b. Would you <u>like to</u> drink something ?

　　Yes, I like to (drink something).

c. Have you cut the grass ?

　　No. I <u>forgot to</u> (cut the grass).

21. 不定詞的時態

A. 現在式——與另外一個動作同時完成。

a. I am trying <u>to finish</u> today's homework.

b. They hoped <u>to join</u> us for dinner.

c. He will call <u>to ask</u> you for some advice.

B. 完成式——比另外一個動作先完成。

a. We are happy <u>to have met</u> you.

b. He seems <u>to have been</u> ill.

c. He claims <u>to have seen</u> a flying saucer.

22. 使用現在式不定詞，卻有指定未來發生的狀態。

a. He intended <u>to write</u> to us.

b. I expect <u>to be</u> there in an hour.

c. I hope <u>to see</u> you again.

23. 不可使用不定詞在有 that 的附屬子句中。

a. I expect <u>that</u> everyone <u>to remain</u> seated. (錯誤)

　　I expect <u>that</u> everyone <u>will remain</u> seated. (正確)

b. I promise <u>that</u> I <u>to return</u> your bicycle in good condition. (錯誤)

　　I promise <u>to return</u> your bicycle in good condition. (正確)

24. 不可使用完成式不定詞，在有過去式或過去完成式之主要動詞之後。

a. The dancers were upset because they had planned <u>to have performed</u> for us. (非正式)

　　The dancers were upset because they had planned <u>to perform</u> for us. (正式)

b. He wanted <u>to have invited</u> all the seniors. (非正式)

　　He wanted <u>to invite</u> all the seniors. (正式)

25. 不定詞的語態

　　A. 現在被動式

　　　a. Cuting grass is going <u>to be done</u> today.

　　　b. Doing homework is going <u>to be finished</u> tomorrow.

　　B. 完成被動式

　　　a. Washing car was going <u>to have been done</u> a few days ago.

　　　b. Painting wall was going <u>to have been finished</u> two days ago.

26. 有些動詞必須用 to 當做它們的補助語，如 agree, care, decide, expect, fail, hope, learn, plan, pretend, promise, refuse, tend, want, wish, etc.

　　　a. We had <u>planned</u> <u>to leave</u> the day before yesterday.

　　　b. Would you <u>care</u> <u>to go</u> to dinner ?

　　　c. Do you <u>wish</u> me <u>to come</u> back later ?

27. 動名詞

　　動名詞是由動詞加上 ing 而成，它不是動詞，而是名詞，但有動詞的意義在內。

　　A. 當主詞用

　　　a. <u>Gardening</u> is my regular work on weekends.

　　　b. <u>Speeding</u> is very important to all drivers.

　　　c. <u>Sleeping</u> well is necessary for our health.

　　B. 當受詞用

　　　a. Do you like <u>cooking</u> ?(動詞的受詞)

　　　b. He suggested <u>painting</u> our house. (動詞的受詞)

　　　c. Don't forget turn on the light before <u>reading</u>. (介詞的受詞)

　　　d. They probably take an hour about <u>walking</u>. (介詞的受詞)

　　C. 當主詞補語用

　　　a. My best <u>habit</u> is <u>getting up early</u>.

　　　b. His <u>relaxation</u> remains <u>fishing for years</u>.

　　D. 當同位語用

　　　a. Mary's <u>job</u>, <u>typing and coping</u>, takes her 5 hours a day.

b. The <u>pastime</u> of Mary's mother, <u>sewing</u>, gives her a lot of fun.

28. 動詞的現在分詞與動名詞不可混淆。

a. They <u>are watching</u> a lot of birds. (是動詞現在進行式)

b. <u>Watching</u> birds in the sky is very interesting. (現在分詞當形容詞)

c. Birds in the zoo are for <u>watching</u>. (動名詞)

29. 動名詞前面要用名詞或代名詞的所有格。

a. His mother agreed to <u>his playing</u> on the piano.

b. The <u>dog's barking</u> at night upset the neighbors.

30. 使用動名詞片語時，要注意主詞與動詞之間的合理性。

a. <u>After receiving the mail</u>, he agreed to cancel the meeting. (合理)

After receiving the mail, the meeting was cancel. (不合理)

b. <u>By running very quick</u>, Frank reached the finish line. (合理)

By running very quick, the finished line was reached. (不合理)

31. 下列這些動詞或動詞片語，必須使用動名詞為補語。

如 admit, appreciate, avoid, be busy, be worth, consider, can't help, complete, deny, enjoy, finish, give up, look, forward to, mind, object to, practice, quit, risk, etc.

a. She is <u>considering</u> not <u>going</u>.

b. I've <u>quit</u> <u>working</u>.

c. Do you <u>object to smoking</u> ?

32. 下列這些動詞或動詞片語，可以使用動名詞或不定詞，但有時候它們的意義會有不同。如 begin, be accustomed to, be worth, while, continue, dislike, forget, forbid, hate, intend, love, prefer, regret, remember, stop, need, tec.

a. His mother forbids him <u>to stay</u> out late on school nights. or

His mother forbids his <u>staying</u> out late on school nights.

b. She prefers <u>to read</u>. Or

She prefers <u>reading</u>.

c. He stopped <u>to smoke</u>. (= He stopped in order to smoke.)

He stopped <u>smoking</u>. (= He didn't smoke any more.)

    d. My pencils needed <u>to be sharpened</u>. Or

    My pencils needed <u>sharpening</u>.

33. 有些普通動詞之後有現在分詞或沒有 to 的不定詞跟隨，雖然現在分詞也是 ing 型式，但它們不是動名詞，因此不可使用所有格。

    a. I heard <u>somebody's knocking</u> at the door. (錯誤)

    I heard <u>somebody knock</u> at the door. (正確)

    b. Did you notice the <u>car's moving</u>？(錯誤)

    Did you notice the <u>car move</u>？(正確)

    Did you notice the <u>car moving</u>？(正確)

34. 現在分詞

動詞加上 ing 而形成，是動詞片語的一部分，可當形容詞，並且有主動的意味。

    A. 當形容詞用——可前位或後位修飾。

      a. This history book is very <u>interesting</u>.

      b. That <u>sleeping</u> baby is my aunt's first kid.

      c. <u>Cutting</u> grass is a hard job.

      d. That's <u>burning</u> warehouse belongs to the local government.

      e. The teacher <u>speaking</u> English is Mrs. Armstrong.

    B. 當補語用——可當主格或受格補語

      a. That <u>big dog</u> went away <u>running</u>.

      b. I saw <u>that dog</u> went away <u>running</u>.

    C. 當現在或過去進行式用。

      a. I'<u>m writing</u> a letter now.

      b. I <u>was writing</u> a letter before he came in the room.

35. 既然動名詞和現在分詞均是由動詞＋ing 而形成，它們如何＋ing 有下列規則。

    A. 大部分的動詞只＋ing 而不做任何改變，如 catch-----catching, enjoy-----enjoying, beat-----beating

B. 假如動詞字尾是 e，要將 e 去掉再＋ing。如 write-----writing, have--
---having, come-----coming

例外一：agree-----agreeing, see-----seeing

例外二：age-----ageing, singe-----singeing

C. 動詞是由一個母音接一個子音，要將子音重複之後再＋ing。

如 sit-----sitting, hit-----hitting, run-----running

D. 兩個音節的動詞，當最後音節要被強調時，要將最後的子音重複
再＋ing。

如 begin-----beginning, upset-----upsetting, forget-----forgetting

例外：如果要被強調的是第一個音節時，不需要將最後子音重
複。

如 profit-----profiting, benefit-----benefiting, differ-----differing

E. 如果動詞的字尾為 ic 時，要將 ic 改成 ick 再＋ing。

如 traffic-----trafficking, panic-----panicking, picnic-----picnicking

F. 其它的動詞還有另外的變化。

如 die-----dying, tie-----tying, lie-----lying

36. 過去分詞

動詞加上 ed 而形成，是動詞片語的一部分，可當形容詞，並且有被動
的意味。

A. 當主格補語用

a. I was surprised at our president's death.

b. My co-worker will get married soon.

B. 當受格補語用

a. I saw a little boy fallen.

b. I got my van painted.

C. 當形容詞用

a. That painted house looks great.

b. This typped paper is his final report.

37. 動詞的單數在下列三種狀況時使用。

A. 數量名詞時

    a. <u>Two weeks</u> never <u>seems</u> long enough for vacation.

    b. <u>Seventy-five cents</u> <u>is</u> not enough for lunch now.

B. 書名，組織，或者國家，它們雖然是複數型態時。

    a. <u>The United States of America</u> <u>is</u> a big country.

    b. <u>Lost Pony Tracks</u> <u>is</u> a book about an Easterner who moved to a ranch in the west.

C. 一些名詞的型態即使是複數時。

    a. <u>Mathematics</u> <u>seems</u> very easy to you and your brother.

    b. <u>Civics</u> <u>is</u> being taught by Ms. Lee.

    c. <u>Mumps</u> <u>is</u> certainly an uncomfortable disease.

    d. No <u>news</u> <u>is</u> good news.

38. 動詞的變化

由於動作的先後或主動被動，因而使得動詞的型態產生變化。

A. 規則動詞的過去式和過去分詞是在原型普通動詞加 ed 或 d。如果動詞的最後字母之前的字母是母音時，要將最後的字母重複之後，再加上 ed 而完成。

原型	現在分詞	過去式	過去分詞
clean	cleaning	cleaned	cleaned
inspect	inspecting	inspected	inspected
like	liking	liked	liked
hop	hopping	hopped	hopped
skip	skipping	skipped	skipped

B. 不規則動詞的過去式和過去分詞往往不同。

    a. 改變母音

原型	現在分詞	過去式	過去分詞
ring	ringing	rang	rung
come	coming	came	come

| shrink | shrinking | shrank | shrunk |

b. 改變母音和子音

原型	現在分詞	過去式	過去分詞
do	doing	did	done
go	going	went	gone
see	seeing	saw	seen
take	taking	took	taken
wear	wearing	wore	worn
write	writing	wrote	written

c.三個時態完全相同

原型	現在分詞	過去式	過去分詞
bet	betting	bet	bet
cost	costing	cost	cost
cut	cutting	cut	cut
let	letting	let	let
read	reading	read	read

39. 動詞的時態

說明動作的時間，是現在，過去，還是未來，以及是在進行或是已經完成。

A. 簡單式——

a.現在簡單式——用現在式動詞

He rings the bell.

b.過去簡單式——用過去式動詞

He rang the bell.

c.未來簡單式——用 shall 或 will 加原型動詞

He will ring the bell.

B. 完成式——

a.現在完成式——has 或 have 加過去分詞

He has rung the bell.

b.過去完成式——had 加過去分詞

He had rung the bell.

c.將來完成式——shall 或 will 加 have 再加過去分詞

He will have rung the bell.

C. 進行式——

a.現在簡單進行式——is 或 are 加現在分詞

He is ringing the bell.

b.過去簡單進行式——was 或 were 加現在分詞

He was ringing the bell.

c.未來簡單進行式——shall 或 will 加 be 再加現在分詞

He will be ringing the bell.

D. 完成進行式——

a.現在完成進行式——has 或 have 加 been 再加現在分詞

He has been ringing the bell.

b.過去完成進行式——had 加 been 加現在分詞

He had been ringing the bell.

c.未來完成進行式——shall 或 will 加 have 加 been 再加現在分詞

He will have been ringing the bell.

40. 動作動詞才能用進行式，反之不是動作動詞就不能用進行式。

如 need, prefer, like, etc.

a. I am needing a car. (不合理)

I need a car. (合理)

b. I am liking this picture. (不合理)

I like this picture. (合理)

c. I am preferring coffee than tea. (不合理)

I prefer coffee than tea. (合理)

41. 動詞的時態在句子中要前後一致，不可隨意的將另外一個動詞改成不同的時態。

    a. He <u>stands</u> on the mound and <u>stared</u> at the batter. (非標準)

       He <u>stands</u> on the mound and <u>stares</u> at the batter. (標準)

    b. I <u>regretted</u> that I <u>chose</u> such a broad topic for my report. (非標準)

       I <u>regretted</u> that I <u>had chosen</u> such a broad topic for my report. (標準)

42. 現在分詞和過去分詞均可當做形容詞用，因此它們在句子當中是何種角色，不可混淆。

    a. The astronaut, <u>floating</u> in space, repaired the satellite. (現在分詞)

    b. The captain <u>is checking</u> the weather forecast. (動詞進行式)

    c. <u>Repaired</u> by the astronaut, the satellite again sent back to the earth. (過去分詞)

    d. The burglar was startled whom he <u>was discovered</u> by the guard. (動詞被動式)

43. 動詞時態的用法

    A. 現在式──它們是被用在表達現在的動作，每天的或者是表達一般的事實。

    a. He <u>owns</u> three calculator.

    b. My son <u>is</u> in the chess club.

    c. The sun <u>rises</u> in the east.

    B. 過去式──它們被用在表達過去的動作，而那個動作並未一直延續到現在。

    a. I <u>went</u> to see my grandmother yesterday.

    b. He <u>read</u> a lot of magazines last year.

    c. We <u>saw</u> her the day before yesterday.

    C. 未來式──它們被用在將來才會發生的動作。

    a. I <u>shall read</u> a lot of books.

    b. They say that it <u>will rain</u>.

    D. 現在進行式──它們被用在說話當下正在發生的動作。

a. I'm teaching English in the class.

b. We are rehearsing the play in the gynasium.

E. 過去進行式——它們被用在強調過去持續進行的動作。

a. She was thinking about the accident all night long.

b. My sister was reading that book all afternoon.

c. He was typing the report when the phone rang.

F. 未來進行式——它們就像現在進行式，有關單一而短暫持續的動作，只不過是發生在將來。

a. That store will be closing soon.

b. I shall be arriving at home tomorrow.

G. 現在完成式－它們被用在表達過去已經發生，而且沒有特定時間完成的動作。

a. One of my friends has visited Taiwan.

b. I have worked there several years.

c. They have bought a new car.

H. 過去完成式——它們被用在表達過去已經完成的動作，而這個動作是發生在其它某些動作或事件之前。

a. When he had washed the dishes, he sat down to rest.

b. After she had revised her essay, she handed it in.

c. She had already put away her winter clothes when an unreasonable cold spell forced her to take them out again.

I. 未來完成式——它們被用在表達一個動作將來會完成，而這個完成的動作是在其它某些動作或事件之前。

a. When I am eighteen, I will have gotten a driver's license.

b. By the time I leave, I shall have packed all my clothes.

c. When he retires from his work, he will have made more than a million dollars.

J. 現在完成進行式——它們被用在表達一個動作過去已經發生，而這個動作卻持續進行到現在。

a. He <u>has been working</u> for the same company for 20 years.

b. I <u>have been playing</u> guitar for six months.

K. 過去完成進行式——它們被用在表達一個動作過去已經發生，而這個動作卻在某些動作或事件之前持續進行。

a. I <u>had been studying</u> English for 10 years before I <u>came</u> to the United States.

b. They <u>had been discussing</u> several important matters before I <u>got</u> there.

L. 未來完成進行式——它們被用在表達一個動作過去已經發生，而這個動作持續進行到現在，卻在將來才會完成。

a. By next month, we <u>shall have been learning</u> English for five years.

b. At the end of next year, they <u>will have been going</u> to school for nine years.

44. 過去發生的兩個動作或事件，我們如果不在乎發生的先後，就用簡單的過去式去表達。

a. I <u>bought</u> some fences and <u>constructed</u> my garden.

b. When he <u>came</u> home, his wife <u>cooked</u> fish and eggs.

45. 在完成式的句子中，碰到第二個動詞的助動詞同為 has，have 或 had 時，可以省略掉。

a. The thief <u>had</u> broken the door and (had) stolen the money.

b. My father <u>has</u> put on the jacket and (has) walked dog to the park.

46. 動詞表達未來的動作，而在一些特定的字或片語之後時，只用現在式簡單動詞。

如 when, before, after, as soon as, whenever, until, etc.

a. Before I <u>lock</u> the doors, I will make certain that all of the lights have been turned off. (不可使用 will lock)

b. Unless Sung <u>passes</u> his chemistry course, he won't graduate this semester. (不可使用 will pase)

c. As soon as he <u>sells</u> his old house, he can buy a new house. (不可使用 will sell)

47. 過去發生的兩個動作或事件，如果我們要強調它們先後次序時，先發生的使用過去完成式，而後發生的則使用過去式。

    a. I <u>constructed</u> my garden after I <u>had bought</u> some fences.

    b. When he <u>came</u> home, his wife <u>had cooked</u> fish and eggs.

48. 動詞的語氣——動詞陳述動作的方法。

  A. 直說法——陳述事實或表達疑問。

    a. He is a good boy.

      Is he a good boy ?

    b. My sister is at home.

      Is your sister at home ?

    c. It is raining now.

      Is it raining now ?

    d. She is a good lady.

      Is she a good lady ?

  B. 命令法——表達命令，請求，禁止等等。

    a. 用原型動詞

      * Stand up!

      * come here John !

      * Put your cup on the table.

    b. 用原型 Be 動詞＋形容詞

      * Be careful !

      * Be quiet !

      * Be honest !

    c. 用 do 加強語氣

      * Do give me a dollar.

      * Do go over there.

      * Do tell him about the accident.

    d. 用否定詞

      * Don't tell him about me.

    * Don't you mind ?

    * Never mind.

e. 用 let ＋受詞＋原型動詞

    * Let me see.

    * Let him tell us the truth.

    * Don't let the dog go out.

C. 假設法——表達願望，假定，非事實等等。

  a. 現在非事實

    If ＋動詞過去式，主詞＋ should, would, could, night ＋原型動詞

    * If I had a bike, I should be very happy.

    * If I were a butterfly, I could go everywhere.

    * I could go everywhere if I were a butterfly. (注意無標點符號)

    * If it snowed in the middle of the summer, all the flowers would die.

    * If you listened more, you would learn what the problems are.

    * If we studied together, we could prepare our homework more easily.

    * I wish I knew what to do in this situation.

  b. 過去非事實

    If ＋動詞過去完成式，主詞＋ should, would, might, could ＋完成式動詞

    * If I had had a millionaire, I should have bought this beautiful house.

    * If it had not got typhoon, we might have gone to hike.

    * We might have gone to hike if it had not got typhoon. (注意無標點符號)

    * If I had known, I wouldn't have said anything.

    * If I had received an invitation, I would have gone with you to the party.

    * If it had not rained so hard, we would have been able to make the trip.

    * I wish yesterday had been Saturday, I would not have had to work,

and I could have gone to the beach.

　　c. 未來非事實

　　　If＋were to＋原型動詞，主詞＋should, would, could, might＋原型
　　　動詞

　　　* If I were to go Taiwan, I would go to Taipei.

　　　* I would go to Taipei if I were to go Taiwan (注意無標點符號)

　　　* If I were to go abroad, I would go to Europe.

　　　* If he were not to pass the examination, what might he do？

　　d. 未來不確定

　　　If ＋ should ＋ 原 型 動 詞 ， 主 詞 shall(should), will(would),
　　　May(might), can(could)＋原型動詞

　　　* If it should get typhoon tomorrow, we will (would) not go to hike.

　　　* We will (would) not go to hike if it should get typhoon tomorrow.

　　　* If she should fail, what should she do？

　　　* If it should rain the day after tomorrow, I will not go to see you.

　　　* If your mother should call, I would tell her to wait a few minutes.

　　e. 未來有可能

　　　If＋原型動詞，主詞＋shall, will, can, may＋原型動詞

　　　* If I have enough time, I shall go to see my grandparents.

　　　* If I study hard, I shall pass my national examination.

　　　* If you do not study hard, you will not pass your examination.

　　　* If he eats too much, he will get sick.

　　　* If it rains, you may get wet.

49. 現在假設是被用在特定且較正式的場合。

　A. 下列動詞被用在 that 子句之前時，that 子句的動詞要用原型。

　　如 advise, ask, command, demand, desire, insist, order, prefer,
　　recommend, require, request, suggest, urge, etc.

　　a. I insisted that he leave.

　　b. The doctor suggested that she not smoke.

c. The judge ordered that the tenants <u>be</u> allowed to stay.

B. 下列名詞被用在 that 子句之前時，that 子句的動詞用原型。

如 recommendation, requirement, suggestion, wish, etc.

a. The <u>recommentation</u> that you <u>be</u> evaluated was approved.

b. The teacher complied with the <u>requirement</u> that all students in education <u>write</u> a report.

c. I have one <u>wish</u> ----- that I <u>be</u> president some day.

C. 下列形容詞被用在 that 子句之前時，that 子句的動詞要用原型。

如 essential, imperative, important, necessary, urgent, etc.

a. It is <u>important</u> that the document <u>be</u> verified.

b. It is <u>imperative</u> that you <u>be</u> on time to go to school.

D. 有些習慣片語要用原型動詞。

如 had better, would rather, etc.

a. She <u>had better</u> not do it.

b. He <u>would rather</u> <u>play</u> tennis than <u>swim</u>.

50. 假設語氣的 were 和其它動詞的過去式，如果所陳述的事與事實相反，
而且是在 if，as if，as though，等等之後和表示一種期望時使用。

a. <u>If</u> he <u>were</u> to proofread his papers he would make fewer errors.

b. On a bad telephone connection, it sometimes sounds <u>as though</u> the caller <u>were</u> ten thousand .miles, away.

c. It isn't as <u>if</u> she <u>had</u> no money.

d. I <u>wish</u> my aunt <u>were</u> here for the holidays.

51. 動詞的語態

動作的發動者是自願還是被迫，它們所組成的句子，就分成主動構句
和被動構句。

A. 主動構句——主詞是動作的發動者，因此動作動詞是主動的狀
態。動作在強調主詞或行為者，比較不強調它們的動作。

a. He <u>throws</u> the stone to the pond.

b. Mary <u>reads</u> a lot of books every night before going to sleep.

c. The fatal fire <u>burned</u> the entire house and <u>killed</u> two people.

d. We <u>will pay</u> back the money next month.

B. 被動構句——某件事或動作被發動者完成，而且強調那件事或動作，而不是強調動作者。

a. The television <u>was turned</u> off by my dad.

b. The car <u>was pulled</u> out of the ditch by the tow truck.

c. English <u>is spoken</u> by most Americans.

52. Be going to＋原型動詞，表示某些動作或事件將來會發生。

a. We <u>are going to get up</u> early tomorrow and go fishing.

b. They <u>are going to tear down</u> that whole block of buildings.

c. Andrew <u>is going to take</u> an examination on Wednesday.

53. 被動語態的時態

一個句子裡如有直接受詞和間接受詞時，任何一個都可以當做被動語態的主詞。通常行動者為主詞時是用主動構句，反之接受者為主詞時是用被動構句。

A. 現在簡單被動式——

am, is, are＋過去分詞

a. I'<u>m punished</u> by my father.

b. Chinese <u>is</u> not <u>taught</u> in our high school.

c. We <u>are taught</u> English by Mr. Lee.

B. 過去簡單被動式——

was, were＋過去分詞

a. The leaky pipe <u>was fixed</u> by the plumber.

b. In the novel the secrets <u>were stolen</u> by the spy.

c. The police <u>were informed</u> of his whereabouts.

C. 未來簡單被動式——

shall be, will be＋過去分詞

a. I <u>shall be taught</u> by Mr. Lee next semester.

b. My shoes <u>will be repaired</u> by him.

c. Some water <u>will be brought</u> from the well.

D. 現在進行被動式——

am, is, are＋being＋過去分詞

a. I'<u>m being taught</u> Japanese by my tutor.

b. A new department store <u>is being built</u> in Washington, D.C. right now.

c. They <u>are being raised</u> here.

E. 過去進行被動式——

was, were＋being＋過去分詞

a. I <u>was being taught</u> to ride a bike by my brother.

b. He <u>was being sent</u> to school.

c. Those classrooms <u>were being cleaned</u> by us then.

F. 現在完成被動式——

has, have been＋過去分詞

a. My shoes <u>have been repaired</u> by John.

b. The child <u>has been found</u> by them at last.

c. Everyone <u>has been asked</u> the same question.

G. 過去完成被動式——

had been＋過去分詞

a. The ship <u>had been sunk</u> by the enemy.

b. The meeting <u>had not been canceled</u> by ten o'clock.

c. All the tickets <u>had been sold</u> many days ago.

H. 未來完成被動式——

shall have, will have＋been＋過去分詞

a. We <u>shall have been taught</u> mathematics for four years by our tutor.

b. That house <u>will have been burnt</u> by the time the firemen yet there.

c. That room <u>will have been painted</u> by five o'clock this afternoon.

54. 儘量使用主動句，少用被動句，因為主動句簡短而有力。尤其是要小心的使用被動句，更不可使用軟弱的，笨拙的，或者困惑的被動句型。

a. The event <u>was completed</u> when a triple somersault <u>was done</u> by Mr. Lee. (軟弱的被動句)

Mr. Lee completed the event by doing triple somersault. (較佳)

b. Steady rains <u>were hoped</u> for by all of us, but a hurricane was wanted by none of us. (弱的被動句)

All of us hoped for steady rains, but none of us wanted a hurricane. (較佳)

c. Those who help themselves <u>are helped</u> by Gold. (弱的被動句)

God helps those who help themselves. (較佳)

55. 下列這些動詞要用主動式，不要用被動式。

如 appear, disappear, happen, occur, seem, take place, etc.

a. He <u>appeared</u> to be happy when he could go out. (正確)

He <u>was appeared</u> to be happy when he could go out. (錯誤)

b. The wild rabit <u>disappeared</u> in our backyard just in a second. (正確)

The wild rabit <u>was disappeared</u> in our backyard just in a second. (錯誤)

c. The car accident <u>occurred</u> before the police came. (正確)

The car accident <u>was occurred</u> before the police came. (錯誤)

56. 動作者是誰不知道或者不讓人知道時，可用被動式。

a. Some defects have been made about our new roof. (正確)

Our new roof has made some defects. (錯誤)

b. A lot of wrong spellings were found in this composition. (正確)

This composition found a lot of wrong spellings. (錯誤)

57. 有些介詞可以代替 by 造成句子的被動式。

a. His coming surprised me. (主動)

I was <u>surprised at</u> his coming. (被動)

b. Many Chinese histories interested lots of foreigners. (主動)

Lots of foreigners were <u>interested in</u> many Chinese histories. (被動)

58. 據說，聽說，人們說等等有人或大家的意思，其主詞往往是 people，

they，we，you，somebody，etc，而它們的句型是被動式時，主詞可以省略掉。

    a. They speak Chinese in China. (主動)

       Chinese are spoken in China. (被動)

    b. People said that Chinatown is very big in New York. (主動)

       Chinatown is very big in New York. (被動)

    c. Somebody stole his new car last month. (主動)

       His new car was stolen last month. (被動)

59. "Do"在命令法的使用規則

  A. 強調特殊的願望，忍耐，說服等等。

    a. Do have another cup of tea.

    b. Do stop talking.

    c. Do help me with this math problem.

  B. 對於要求或提供的反應等等，這時 do 和 don't 可以代替整個命令的狀態。

    a. May (or Shall) I switch the light off ?

       Yes, do.　or No, don't

    b. Can I leave right now ?

       Yes, do.　or No, don't.

60. "Have", "Have got"或減縮成"got"不管在現在式或過去式的使用規則。

  A. 在擁有或持有時──

    I have (got) a new house.

  B. 在能夠提供的意念時──

    a. Do you have (got) any ink ?

    b. Have you (got) any ink ?

    c. You let me have some ?

       均可答 Yes, I can.

  C. 在確定的物品或物質數量時──

a. I have (got) fourteen pencils.

b. I have (got) a lot of milk.

D. 在身體上的特有現象時——

a. He has (got) big brown eyes.

b. Our dog has (got) long hair.

c. Our house has (got) eleven rooms.

E. 在精神上和情緒上與一些名詞連結，再去描述個性時——

a. She has (got) nice manners.

b. Have you (got) any faith in what he tells you？

F. 在家庭的關係上時——

I have (got) 4 brothers.

G. 在與其它人接觸時——

I have (got) a good dentist.

(Whom I can recommend to you.)

H. 在有"wear"的意念時，往往與介詞 on 連結使用。

a. That's a nice hat you have. (You've got.)

b. That's a beautiful tie you have on. (You've got on.)

c. I have (got) nothing on.

I. 在與一些名詞連結而描述疾病時——

a. I have (got) a cold.

b. I have (got) a bad backache.

c. The baby has (got) measles.

J. 在與一些名詞連結而有特殊安排時——

a. My wife has (got) an appointment with her dentist next Saturday morning.

b. Wilson has (got) an interview for a job today.

c. I have (got) a meeting with my boss this afternoon.

K. 在與一些名詞連結而表達意見時——

a. I have (got) an idea.

b. Have you (got) any opinion to this proposal ?

c. He has (got) a point of view about that new garage.

L. 在有"there is"之意念時——

a. You have (got) a stain on your tie. (There is a stain on your tie.)

b. You have (got) sand in your hair. (= There is sand in your hair.)

61. "Have"除了擁有某些東西之外，還有下列之意義。

a.命令的——

* Have a cup of tea !

b.簡單現在式——

* I always have sugar in my coffee.

c.現在進行式——

* We're having a nice holiday.

d.簡單過去式——

* We had a lovely vacation last summer.

e.過去進行式——

* I was having a shower when the phone rang.

f.現在完成式——

* Poor Jack has just had an accident.

g.現在完成進行式——

* The children have been having a lot of fun.

h.過去完成式——

* I woke up early because I had had a bad dream this morning.

i.過去完成進行式——

* I had been having long hair for five years before I came to this school.

j.簡單未來式——

* I'll have a haircut tomorrow.

k.未來進行式——

* If anyone phones, I'll be having a bath.

l.未來完成式——

    * You'll have had an answer by tomorrow.

m.未來完成進行式——

    * She will have been having treatment all her life.

n.和語態動詞連結——could, can, might, may, etc.

    * You could have a cup of orange juice if you like.

62. 變化不完全的動詞

語態動詞有時候被稱為變化不完全動詞，因為它們沒有不定詞和分詞，與一般正常的動詞不同。

  a. 要使用不定詞時，必須使用其它的動詞代替。

    * If you want to apply for this job, you have <u>to be able to</u> type at least 60 words a minute. (正確)

    * If you want to apply for this job, you have <u>to can to</u> type at least 60 words a minute. (錯誤)

  b. 可以使用沒有 to 的不定詞和語態動詞結合。

    * You <u>must not phone</u> him at midnight. (正確)

    * You <u>must not to phone</u> him at midnight. (錯誤)

  c. 可以使用其它動詞來代替沒有 ing 型態的語態動詞。

    * I <u>couldn't go</u> home by bus, so that I took a taxi.

    * I <u>wasn't able to go</u> school on foot, so that I took a school bus.

  d. 不可以在第三人稱單數使用語態動詞亦即＋s 或 es。

    * The boss <u>can</u> see you now. (正確)

    * The boss <u>cans</u> see you now. (錯誤)

  e. 每一個語態動詞都有它自己的基本意義，經過比較之後，有的是當助動詞，有的只有文法上的功能而已。

    * I <u>might</u> see you tomorrow.

    * <u>May</u> I have your name and address？

    * <u>Could</u> you help me please？

63. 表原因的動詞

這種動詞與被動式類似，我們專注在某件工作被某些事物或某些人完成。換句話說，我們是強調使喚某一些人來幫我們完成一件工作。

A. have, make, let, bid＋受詞（人或動物）

　　a. He <u>had</u> me do the work.

　　b. <u>Let</u> John and me do the work.

　　c. He <u>made</u> his wife go home.

　　d. The policeman <u>bade</u> the thief stop.

B. 表原因動詞＋受詞（事物）＋過去分詞

　　a. We <u>have</u> our house <u>painted</u> every year. (現在式)

　　b. We <u>are having</u> our house <u>painted</u> soon. (現在進行式)

　　c. We <u>had</u> our house <u>painted</u> last year. (過去式)

　　d. We <u>have</u> just <u>had</u> our house <u>painted</u>. (現在完成式)

　　e. We <u>will have</u> our house <u>painted</u> next year. (未來式)

　　f. We<u>'ll be having</u> our house <u>painted</u> next year. (未來進行式)

　　g. We <u>may have</u> our house <u>painted</u> next year. (語態型)

　　h. We <u>may be having</u> our house <u>painted</u> soon. (語態型)

C. 表原因動詞＋受詞（人，動物或事物）＋不定詞

　　a. He <u>caused</u> me <u>to come</u> late.

　　b. He <u>got</u> me <u>to do</u> the work.

　　c. His wife was <u>made</u> <u>to go</u> home.

　　d. The thief was <u>bidden</u> <u>to stop</u>.

64. 什麼時候使用否定的疑問句。

　　a. 當我們期待，要求或希望的回答是肯定時

　　　Don't you remember that holiday we had in Europe？　Yes, I do.

　　b. 當我們願望表達驚奇，不信或憤怒時

　　　Can't you ride a bicycle？　No, I can't.

　　c. 當我們願望說服某人時

　　　Won't you help me？　Oh, all right then.　No, I'm afraid I can't.

　　d. 當我們要譴責或表達騷擾或諷刺時

Can't you shut the door behind you？

e. 當我們感嘆某件事時

Didn't he do well！ Isn't it hot in here！

第十章 ｜ 片語（Phrases）

1. 片語

   片語顧名思義就是一群字，被用來談語或寫作的一部分。它們沒有主詞也沒有動詞，因此無法表達完整的意義，它們是被當做修飾語而已。

   A. 形容詞片語——通常是介詞片語當形容詞用。

      a. The students in our school did well on the test.

      b. The elementary school children played soccer.

      c. She likes the skirt with the big pockets.

   B. 副詞片語——可修飾動詞和副詞。

      a. They went to Washington, D.C. the day before yesterday.

      b. Our baseball team played with a lot of energy.

      c. We walk along the lake every Saturday.

   C. 名詞片語——可當主詞和受詞。

      a. I really don't know what to do right now.

      b. Some days Agba received bread and water for supper.

      c. In Seattle, we visited Pioneer Square and Waterfront park.

   D. 動詞片語——當動詞用，同單字動詞

      a. I always look forward to your visits.

      b. Who takes care of your children at day time ?

      c. We have been living in the United States of America for more than thirty years.

   E. 介詞片語——可當形容詞和副詞

      a. I can't read the notice because he's standing in front of it.

b. The house <u>across the street</u> has green shutters.

c. The messenger slipped the note <u>under the door</u>.

F. 現在分詞片語——可當形容詞也是動詞的一部分，因此可以稱為動詞形容詞。

   a. <u>Darting suddenly</u>, the cat escaped through the door.

   b. <u>Watching the clock</u>, the coach became worried.

   c. The coach <u>has been watching</u> the clock.

G. 過去分詞片語——可當形容詞也是動詞的一部分，同樣的也可稱為動詞形容詞。

   a. A <u>peeled and sliced</u> cucumber can be added to a garden salard.

   b. <u>Nominated unanimously</u> by the delegates, the candidate thanked her supporters.

   c. <u>Cheered on</u> by the spectators, the little bay horse swept past the finish line in record time.

H. 動名詞片語——可當主詞，受詞，同位語和主格補語。

   a. <u>Walking on the grass</u> is forbidden everywhere.

   b. I feared <u>skiing vapidly down</u> the mountain.

   c. His job is <u>giving the customers their menus</u>.

I. 不定詞片語——可當形容詞，副詞和名詞

   a. <u>To hit a curve ball solidly</u> is very difficult.

   b. She wants <u>to be a lawyer</u>.

   c. We were asked <u>to examine Maya Angelou's descriptions</u> of her childhood.

J. 沒有 to 的不定詞片語——可當形容詞，副詞和名詞

   a. She helps us <u>see her grandmother's store</u> through the eyes of a fascinated child.

   b. He will help us <u>paddle the canoe</u>.

   c. We don't dare <u>go outside during the storm</u>.

2. 動詞片語形成的方法

a. 動詞＋不定詞

agree to, decide to, expect to, plan to, refuse to, afford to, etc.

b. 動詞＋動名詞

consider＋ing 型動詞，enjoy＋ing 型動詞，keep on＋ing 型動詞，
quit＋ing 型動詞，etc.

c. 動詞＋不定詞或動名詞均可。

begin to or begin＋ing 型動詞，hate to or hate＋ing 型動詞，etc.

d. 動詞 go 有關描述活動時＋動名詞

go fishing, go shopping, go swimming, etc.

第十一章 | 子句 (Clauses) 和句子 (Sentences)

1. 子句雖然是一群字組合而成，但與片語不同，因為子句有主詞和動詞，而且可以表達部分的意思。

A. 獨立子句——有主詞和動詞之外，它們可以完整的表達意思，而且可以單獨存在。

   a. The outfielders were missing easy fly balls.

   b. The infidders were throwing wildly.

   c. The outfielders were missing easy fly balls, and the infidders were throwing wildly.

   d. Should we go for a walk ?

   e. Is it too hot outside ?

   f. Should we go for a walk, or is it too hot outside ?

   g. Gladys was not tired.

   h. Her tennis partner was not tired.

   i. Gladys was not tired, but her tennis partner was.

B. 附屬子句——有主詞和動詞，但不能完整的表達意思，必須與主要子句連結起來，才可以很完整的表達意思。

   a. 名詞子句——當做名詞（主詞，受詞和同位語）

   * Mr. Perkins told us <u>what we would play at half time</u>.

   * We never know <u>whether he will choose a march or a show tune</u>.

   * The crowd always applauds enthusiastically for <u>whoever plays a solo</u>.

   * The question is <u>who will deliver the information</u>.

   * <u>Whatever you decide</u> will be fine with us. （主詞）

* The worst flaw in the story is <u>that it doesn't have a carefully developed plot</u>. (主格補語)

* Do you know <u>what happened to the rest of my tuna fish sandwich</u>? (直接受詞)

* The painter gave <u>whatever spots had dried</u> another coat of enamel. (間接受詞)

* Sue is looking for <u>whoever owns that red bicycle</u>. (介詞的受詞)

b. 副詞子句——當做副詞（修飾動詞，形容詞和副詞）

* Roth mowed the lawn <u>while we weeded the flower beds</u>.

* <u>Until we had pulled out the weeds</u>, we could not see the roses.

* What countries would you visit <u>if you could travel anywhere in the world</u>?

* Give some consideration to these <u>whenever you make your travel plans</u>.

* Long hours in the hot sun had made us feel <u>as though the day would never end</u>.

* <u>As you look into a mirror</u>, your left hand seems to be the image's right hand.

c. 形容詞子句——當做形容詞（修飾名詞或代名詞）

* A speech communities <u>that consist of millions of people and some that contain</u> is a group of people <u>who speak the same language</u>.

* The language <u>that we use during our childhood</u> is called our native language.

* People <u>who conduct business internationally</u> should know more than one language.

* A submarine sailor <u>who looks through a periscope</u> is using a system of lenses and mirrors to see above the water's surface.

* A black hole, <u>which results after a star has collapsed</u>, can trap energy and matter.

* Helen Keller was a remarkable woman <u>who overcame blindness and deafness</u>.

* The problem <u>that worries us now</u> is the pollution of underground sources of water.

2. 獨立子句（或稱主要子句），可以單獨存在成為句子，也可以和另外一個獨立子句連結，更能完整表達意思。

   a. My father drove me to subway station. (句子)

   b. Since I missed the bus, <u>my father drove me to subway station</u>. (獨立子句)

   c. My father drove me to subway station, and I arrived at school on time. (兩個獨立子句)

3. 簡單句——有一個獨立子句，但沒有附屬子句

   a. Our <u>class</u> <u>is writing</u> stories for the second graders at Thomson Elementary School. (一個主詞和一個動詞)

   b. The <u>gymnasts</u> and their <u>coaches</u> performed for the assembly. (複合主詞)

   c. William <u>read</u> The Washington Post and <u>reported</u> on it last week. (複合動詞)

   d. Neither <u>Wilson</u> nor his <u>father</u> <u>has read</u> the book or <u>seen</u> the movie. (複合主詞和動詞)

4. 連合句——有兩個或兩個以上的獨立子句連結，是沒有附屬子句的連結。獨立子句的連結是用對等連接詞，而且要用點號“,”加以分開。

   a. <u>No one was injured in the fire</u>, but <u>several homes were destroyed</u>.

   b. <u>Our landlord is kind</u>, yet <u>he will not allow us to have pets</u>.

   c. <u>They did not watch the shuttle take off</u>, nor <u>did they watch it land</u>. (是否定句，要用倒裝法)

5. 複合句——是由一個獨立子句和一個或一個以上的附屬子句連結。

   a. <u>After she recovered</u>, <u>she could no longer see or hear</u>.

   b. <u>We sat in the balcony</u> <u>when we attended the concert</u>.

c. <u>One interesting event</u> <u>that is held in the Southwest</u> <u>is the annual Inter-tribal Ceremonial</u>, <u>which involves many different Indian tribes</u>.

6. 複連合句——是由兩個或兩個以上的連合句和一個或一個以上的附屬子句連結。

    a. <u>It is true</u> <u>that he is 85 years old</u>, <u>but he is still strong</u>.

    b. <u>There are 50 students</u> <u>who are interested in attending the science fair at the community college</u>, <u>and they should sign up now</u>.

    c. <u>In laboratory studies, scientists have determined</u> <u>that various plants respond differently to increase in carbon dioxide tevels</u>; <u>some plants grow at a faster pace</u>.

7. 修飾用的片語和子句必須儘量靠近所要修飾的字，才能顯示清晰的和有感覺的在修飾那個字。

    a. The hat belongs to me with the feather. (錯亂的)

    The hat <u>with the feather</u> belongs to me. (清晰的)

    b. She read about the new show that had opened in the newspaper. (錯亂的)

    <u>In the newspaper</u>, she read about the show that had opened. (清晰的)

    c. He said in the afternoon he was going to Maryland. (混亂的)

    He said he was going to Maryland <u>in the afternoon</u>. (清晰的)

    <u>In the afternoon</u> he said he was going to Maryland. (清晰的)

    d. Stolen from the media center, the deputies found the video recorder. (搖擺的)

    The deputies found the video recorder <u>stolen from the media center</u>. (修正的)

    e. Sleeping on the roof I saw the neighbor's cat. (搖擺的)

    I saw the neighbor's cat <u>sleeping on the roof</u>. (修正的)

    f. Living by the airport, the noise bothered us. (搖擺的)

    <u>Living by the airport</u>, we were bothered by the noise. (修正的)

    g. The picnic in the park that we had was fun. (錯置的)

The picnic <u>that we had</u> in the park was fun. (修正的)

h. The film was about earthquakes that we saw. (錯置的)

The film <u>that we saw</u> was about earthquakes. (修正的)

i. The cleanup program was supported by the students that the seventh-grade president suggested. (錯置的)

The cleanup program <u>that the seventh-grade president suggested</u> was supported by the students. (修正的)

8. 附屬子句一定不可以當做句子在使用。

a. When it rains during a football game. (片斷)

When it rains during a football game, the stadium looks like a patchwork quilt of umbrella. (句子)

It rains during a football game. (句子)

b. Who directed us to our seats. (片斷)

We found an usher who directed us to our seats. (句子)

An usher directed us to our seats. (句子)

9. 動詞片語一定不可以當做句子在使用。

a. Built of bamboo. (片斷)

A house built of bamboo cannot withstand a heavy wind. (句子)

b. Waiting at the doctor's office. (片斷)

Waiting at the doctor's office is difficult for me. (句子)

10. 同位語一定不可以當做句子在使用。

a. The eighteen sailors rowed 3618 miles to Timor. An island near Java. (片斷)

The eighteen sailors rowed 3618 miles to Timor, an island near Java. (句子)

b. We had dinner at the Banana Tree. A restaurant near Key West. (片斷)

We had dinner at the Banana Tree, a restaurant near Key West. (句子)

11. 連續的句子是包括兩個或兩個以上的句子，只用標點符號分開，甚至沒有標點符號，這些是不正確的使用。

a. The black variety was extremely rare, most people had only seen speckled pepper moths. (連續的句子)

The black variety was extremely rare. Most people had only seen speckled pepper moths. (正確的)

b. The black moths could be easily seen they were frequently killed by birds. (連續的句子)

The black moths could be easily seen. They were frequently killed by birds. (正確的)

12. 要儘量避免使用 and，but，for，nor 等連接詞在黏連而單調的主要子句中。

a. Wilson caught the pass, and he ran twenty-two yards, and so he made a first down. (黏連的)

After he had caught the pass, Wilson ran twenty-two yards, making a first down. (比較好)

b. Juliette went the board, and she drew a map, but her directions were still not clear to the class. (黏連的)

Although Juliette went to the board and drew a map, her directions, were still not clear to the class. (比較好)

13. 一個動詞的主詞絕不要放在修飾用的片語中。修飾用的片語包括一個名詞或代名詞時，它們往往在動詞之前，但是名詞或代名詞跟隨著介詞時，它們並不是主詞。

a. Most of the women voted. (錯誤)

Most women voted. (正確)

b. Around the corner from here is a store. (錯誤)

A store is around the corner from here. (正確)

14. 連合主詞包括兩個或兩個以上的主詞，藉由連接詞連結時，它們可以有共同的動詞。

a. Moles and bats supposedly have very poor eyesight.

b. There are a dozen eggs and a pound of butter left.

15. 平行的構句

為了有效的寫作，讓句子用平行的安排，用相同的文法格式，去強調
理念同樣的重要。

  a. 名詞對名詞

    * My daughter liked mathematical research more than to supervise a large laboratory. (錯誤的)

    * My daughter liked mathematical <u>research</u> more than <u>supervision</u> a large laboratory. (平行的)

  b. 不定詞對不定詞

    * The suggestion was to skim and then scanning for information. (錯誤的)

    * The suggestion was <u>to skim</u> and then <u>to scan</u> for information. (平行的)

  c. 行動動詞對行動動詞

    * He reads a newspaper, makes a phone call, types a report, and a letter is mailed this morning. (錯誤的)

    * He <u>reads</u> a newspaper, <u>makes</u> a phone call, <u>types</u> a report and <u>mail</u> a letter this morning. (平行的)

  d. 介詞對介詞

    * English seems a more difficult subject for boys than girls. (錯誤的)

    * English seems a more difficult subject <u>for boys</u> than <u>for girls</u>. (平行的)

  e. 動名詞對動名詞

    * In the autumn I enjoy playing soccer and to take long walks in the woods. (錯誤的)

    * In the autumn I enjoy <u>playing</u> soccer and <u>taking</u> long walks in the woods. (平行的)

  f. 形容詞對形容詞

    * There are twenty-five, large, round, red, and made of wood tables in

the restaurant. (錯誤的)

> * There are <u>twenty-five</u>, <u>large</u>, <u>round</u>, <u>red</u>, and <u>wooden</u> tables in the restaurant. (平行的)

g. 關係連接詞對關係連接詞

> * He enjoyed not only the movie and the play. (錯誤的)
>
> * He enjoyed <u>not only</u> the movie <u>but also</u> the play. (平行的)

h. 關係結構對關係結構

> * Both the slecting and to purchase were his jobs. (錯誤的)
>
> * <u>Both the selecting</u> <u>and the purchasing</u> were his jobs. (平行的)

i. 子句對子句

> * That you learn responsibility is as important as doing your schoolwork. (錯誤的)
>
> * <u>That you learn responsibility</u> is as important as <u>that you do your schoolwork</u>. (平行的)

16. 連合動詞包括兩個或兩個以上的動詞，用連接詞連結時，必須用同一個主詞。

a. <u>Will</u> <u>you</u> <u>walk</u> home or <u>wait</u> for the four o'clock bus ?

b. <u>The newborn calf</u> <u>rose</u> to its feet with a wobbling motion and <u>stood</u> for the first time.

17. 在正式的寫作裡，要避免使用不確定的代名詞，如 it，they 和 you 等等。

a. In the paper <u>it</u> said that a vocano erupted in the Indian Ocean. (不確定)

The newspaper reported that a vocano erupted in the Indian Ocean. (比較好)

b. They had whirled so fast <u>it</u> made them dizzy. (不確定)

They had whirled so fast that they were dizzy. (比較好)

c. In some nineteenth century novels <u>you</u> are always meeting difficult words. (不確定)

In some nineteenth century novel the vocabulary is quite difficult. (比較好)

18. 為了避免句子冗長，經由子句改成片語，或片語改成單字的方法達成。

A. 子句減少成分詞，動名詞或不定詞片語

    a. <u>When they were trapped by a cave-in</u>, the miners waited for rescuers. (子句)

    <u>Trapped by a cave-in</u>, the miners waited for rescuers. (分詞片語)

    b. <u>Because we had found no one home</u>, we left a note. (子句)

    <u>Having found no one home</u>, we left a note. (分詞片語)

    c. <u>If you leave at noon</u>, you can get to Chicago at three o'clock. (子句)

    <u>Leaving at noon</u> will get you to Chicago at three o'clock. (動名詞片語)

    d. We decided <u>that we would get an early start</u>. (子句)

    We decided <u>to get an early start</u>. (不定詞片語)

B. 子句減少成修飾的片語

    a. The teams <u>that had come from Missourie</u> were not scheduled to play the first day of the tournament. (子句)

    The teams <u>from Missourie</u> were not scheduled to play the first day of the tournament. (片語)

    b. <u>When the sun sets</u>, the streetlights come on. (子句)

    <u>At sunset</u> the streetlights come on. (片語)

C. 子句減少成同位語

    a. Dr. Brown, <u>who is the chief surgeon</u>, will operate. (子句)

    Dr. Brown, <u>the chief surgeon</u>, will operate. (同位語)

    b. Her two days, <u>one of which is a collie and the other a spaniel</u>, perform different duties on the farm. (子句)

    Her two days, <u>a collie and a spaniel</u> perform different duties on the farm. (同位語)

D. 子句和片語減少成單字

    a. The dance classes <u>that have been canceled</u> will be rescheduled. (子句)

    The <u>canceled</u> dance classes will be rescheduled. (單字)

    b. Laura is a runner <u>who never tires</u>. (子句)

    Laura is a <u>tireless</u> runner. (單字)

    c. Her career <u>in the movie</u> was brief. (片語)

    Her <u>movie</u> career was brief. (單字)

    d. She greeted everyone <u>in a cordial manner</u>. (片語)

    She greeted everyone <u>cordially</u>. (單字)

19. 避免重複

A. 避免使用相同意義的字，繼續不斷的在句子中。

    a. The money that I have is <u>sufficient enough</u> for my tuition. (不正確)

    The money that I have is <u>enough</u> for my tuition. (正確)

    The money that I have is <u>sufficient</u> for my tuition. (正確)

    b. The book is <u>free gratis</u>. (不正確)

    The book is <u>free</u>. (正確)

    The book is <u>gratis</u>. (正確)

B. 避免使用名詞和代名詞有關它們的時候，繼續不斷的在句子中。

    a. <u>Judy she</u> plans to go into business with her friend. (不正確)

    <u>Judy</u> plans to go into business with her friend. (正確)

    b. <u>Jiun he</u> wants to visit Washington, D.C. before he goes New York. (不正確)

    <u>Jiun</u> wants to visit Washington, D.C. before he goes New York. (正確)

20. 避免遺漏

A. 不要遺漏名詞前面必要的冠詞。

    a. It was so pleasant <u>day</u> that we sat on the patio for hours. (錯誤)

    It was so pleasant <u>a day</u> that we sat on the patio for hours. (正確)

    b. The morning newspaper is <u>on table</u>. (錯誤)

    The morning newspaper is <u>on the table</u>. (正確)

B. 不要遺漏必要的介詞

　　a. I run into him <u>time to time</u>. (錯誤)

　　　I run into him <u>from time to time</u>. (正確)

　　b. The thing that I was most <u>surprised</u> was his attitude. (錯誤)

　　　The thing that I was most <u>surprised at</u> was his attitude. (正確)

C. 不要遺漏必要的代名詞

　　a. The problem was a complex one, so we needed ample time to discuss. (錯誤)

　　　The problem was a complex one, so we needed ample time to discuss it. (正確)

　　b. Since it was <u>vacation</u>, it should be their decision how to spend it. (錯誤)

　　　Since it was <u>their vacation</u>, it should be their decision how to spend it. (正確)

D. 不要遺漏重要的主詞

　　a. I'll meet him when <u>comes</u>. (錯誤)

　　　I'll meet him when <u>he comes</u>. (正確)

　　b. I have never seen such a man <u>as</u>. (錯誤)

　　　I have never seen such a man <u>as he</u>. (正確)

E. 不要遺漏"that"在附屬子句中，以免造成讀者對句子的誤解。

　　a. It is belived, especially in the capital, <u>the government</u> is gaining strength. (錯誤)

　　　It is belived, especially in the capital, <u>that the government</u> is gaining strength. (正確)

　　b. <u>The research</u> had been easy astounded him. (錯誤)

　　　<u>That the research</u> had been easy astounded him. (正確)

F. 不要遺漏動詞或重要的動詞一部分。

　　a. They took the steps because of the elevator, which <u>broken</u>. (錯誤)

　　　They took the steps because of the elevator, which <u>was broken</u>. (正確)

b. I wanted her to help me, but she must not have <u>wanted</u>. (錯誤)

I wanted her to help me, but she must not have <u>wanted to</u>. (正確)

G. 不要遺漏做標誌的人或物（關係代名詞）

a. The <u>book</u> was required reading was being held at the reference desk. (錯誤)

The <u>book which</u> was required reading was being held at reference desk. (正確)

b. The <u>people</u> cheated on the examination had to leave the room. (錯誤)

The <u>people who</u> cheated on the examination had to leave the room. (正確)

H. 在比較的時候不可遺漏需要的字，換句話說，要清楚的描述什麼東西在比較。

a. The average temperature in Dallas is higher <u>than</u> New York. (不清楚)

The average temperature in Dallas is higher <u>than that in</u> New York. (清楚)

b. The hide of the rhinoceros is harder <u>than</u> the alligator. (不清楚)

The hide of the rhinoceros is harder <u>than that of</u> the alligator. (清楚)

I. 不要遺漏"other"或"else"當比較一件事物，在一整個群體之中是一部分時。

a. Our school is larger than <u>any</u> in the city. (荒謬的)

Our school is larger than <u>any other</u> in the city. (合理的)

b. Jan is funnier than <u>anybody</u> in her class. (荒謬的)

Jan is funnier than <u>anybody else</u> in her class. (合理的)

J. 不要遺漏冠詞，介詞或代名詞在平行建構句中，無論如何有必要使得意義更清晰。

a. Winning the Westinghouse Scholarship was as great a pleasure to the teacher as <u>the student</u>. (模糊的)

Winning the Westinghouse Scholarship was as great a pleasure to the teacher as <u>to the students</u>. (清晰的)

b. After the celebration we were introduced to the president <u>and</u> master of ceremonies. (模糊的)

After the celebration we were introduced to the president <u>and to the</u> master of ceremonies. (清晰的)

21. 字的順序

字的順序是非常有彈性的，它們的位置常常是可以改變的。

A. 主詞和動詞

在陳述語氣中，主詞永遠在動詞之前。相反的，在問句中，則動詞在主詞之前。

a. Bill made a statement about the university. (肯定句)

b. Mark hasn't touched a book since the semester began. (否定句)

c. What is the woman trying to do？(疑問句)

B. 冠詞，形容詞和名詞

冠詞永遠在名詞，所有代名詞，指示代名詞和不確定代名詞之前。形容詞通常在名詞之前，如果形容詞有兩個或兩個以上形容同一個名詞時，它們的順序是數量形容詞在前，其後為修飾形容詞，顏色有關的形容詞，最後為形容詞的相等語。

a. Those seven small old stone houses were built in 1880.

b. She sent her nice blue silk dress to the laundry.

C. 副詞

在正常狀態下，多數副詞都在句尾。狀態副詞最先，其次為地方副詞，第三為頻率副詞，最後為時間副詞。副詞在形容詞或動詞之後，頻率為時間副詞。副詞在形容詞或動詞之後，頻率副詞在主要動詞之前，但在"be"動詞之後。

a. He spent three hours in the library <u>yesterday</u>.

b. He looked <u>everywhere</u> for the lost dog.

c. I don't know him <u>well enough</u> to borrow money from him.

d. I have been to the United States several times <u>this</u> year.

e. We have <u>often</u> visited our grandparents.

f. Our teacher are <u>always</u> <u>on time</u>.

D. 疑問代名詞

在名詞子句中，如果是以疑問字介紹時，則用陳述句的字序。

a. I'm not sure what he bought at the store.

b. Do you know who he is the right man?

E. 倒裝句

當一個句子是用否定或近乎否定的字或片語開頭時，用疑問句的字序。在條件句中，我們也是要使用問句的字序，但必須將"if"省略掉。

a. Never in my life have I heard or seen such a thing.

b. Not only did he cut two trees, but also he left the yard messed.

c. No sooner had I left my house than it began to rain.

d. Had I been there, I would help you.

e. Were I rich, I would buy a big and beautiful house.

f. Had I had time last summer, I would have taken a long vacation.

第十二章 | 一致性（Agreement）

1. 主詞和動詞的一致
   A. 主詞如果是複數，動詞必須用複數，主詞如果是單數，動詞則必須為單數。
      a. <u>Squirrels</u> <u>eat</u> the seeds from the bird feeder.
      b. One <u>exhibit</u> <u>provides</u> an experience with complete darkness.
      c. <u>Visitors</u> <u>walk</u> through a tunnel with no light at all.
      d. Thirty <u>students</u> <u>are</u> going on the field trip.
   B. 主詞的單複數不因為有片語的跟隨而改變。
      a. <u>Industries</u> in the community <u>have</u> (not has) suffered in recent years.
      b. However, their <u>search</u> for leftovers <u>creates</u> (not create) problem for Kodiak.
      c. One <u>cannery</u> on the island <u>cans</u> (not can) delicious salmon.
   C. 當兩個主詞由連接詞"and"連結時，即使各個主詞為單數，這個句子的動詞仍為複數。
      a. A desk and a bookcase <u>were</u> (not was)
         moved into my younger brother's bedroom.
      b. Mosquitoes and earwigs <u>have</u> (not has) invaded our back yard.
2. 時態的一致
   不要任意的，不需要的去改變句中從一個時態到另外一個時態。
      a. He <u>stands</u> on the mound and <u>stared</u> at the batter. (非標準的)
         He <u>stands</u> on the mound and <u>stares</u> at the batter. (標準的)
      b. I <u>regretted</u> that I <u>chose</u> such a broad topic for my report. (非標準的)
         I <u>regretted</u> that I <u>had chosen</u> such a broad topic for my report. (標準

的)

3. 肯定的一致

避免使用 also 代替 so，避免使用 be 代替 do，避免重複使用動詞去代替 do，以及避免使用錯誤的型態。

    a. They were surprised, and <u>also were we</u>. (不正確)

       They were surprised, and <u>we were so</u>. (不正確)

       They were surprised, and <u>so were we</u>. (正確)

    b. My wife wanted to go home, and <u>so were I</u>. (不正確)

       My wife wanted to go home, <u>so wanted I</u>. (不正確)

       My wife wanted to go home, and <u>so did I</u>. (正確)

4. 否定的一致

避免使用 either 代替 neither，避免使用 neither 代替 either，避免使用主詞在 be，do，have 或語態動詞之前，而有 neither 的句子中。

    a. If Jane won't go to the party, <u>either</u> will he. (不正確)

       If Jane won't go to the party, <u>neither</u> will he. (正確)

    b. She is not in agreement, and I'm not <u>neither</u>. (不正確)

       She is not in agreement, and I'm not <u>either</u>. (正確)

    c. My roommate hasn't gone, and <u>I have neither</u>. (不正確)

       My roommate hasn't gone, and <u>neither have I</u>. (正確)

5. 複合主詞用 or 或 nor 連結時，動詞必須符合最接近的主詞。

    a. Some new statues <u>or</u> <u>a fountain has</u> (not have) been planned for the park.

    b. Neither the announcer <u>nor</u> <u>the players were</u> (not was) happy with the decision.

    c. Flowers <u>or</u> <u>a colorful picture makes</u> (not make) a room cheerful.

6. 一個句子如果以 there 或 here 開頭時，主詞大概在動詞之後，先找出主詞，然後動詞再配合它。同樣的，在問句中也是如此原則。

    a. There <u>is</u> (not are) a <u>pint</u> of strawberries in the kitchen.

    b. Here <u>is</u> (not are) the overdue <u>book</u> about reptiles.

    c. There <u>are</u> (not is) three foreign exchange <u>students</u> at the high school.

    d. <u>Have</u> (not Has) the <u>sixth-graders</u> elected their officers?

7. 在一個句子中，不可使用雙重否定的字，否則主詞和動詞之間的互動會變成非常混亂。

如 no, not, none, never, no one, nothing, hardly, barely, only, scarcely, etc.

    a. They <u>never</u> ride their bikes on the highway. (正確)

       They <u>never hardly</u> ride their bikes on the highway. (錯誤)

    b. Judy <u>didn't</u> tell <u>anyone</u> about her job. (正確)

       Judy <u>didn't</u> tell <u>no one</u> about her job. (錯誤)

    c. I was so angry that I could <u>hardly</u> speak <u>anything</u>. (正確)

       I was so angry that I could <u>hardly</u> speak <u>nothing</u>. (錯誤)

第十三章 ｜ 容易混淆的字（Common Usage Problems）

1. Its 是 it 的所有格，it's 是 it is 或 it has 的簡寫。

    a. The cat drank <u>its</u> milk and washed <u>its</u> ears.

    b. <u>It's</u> a four hour drive from New York to Washington, D.C.

    c. <u>It's</u> rained.

2. Not 是副詞，當 not 是簡寫的一部分時，如 hadn't，那麼 n't 是副詞，No 是形容詞。

    a. <u>Not</u> everyone likes this book.

    b. I've <u>no</u> time to talk to you just now.

3. Sit 是動詞，它的意義是坐在某個地方，如坐在椅子上，它的詞類變化是 sit，sitting，sat 和 sat。set 也是動詞，它的意義是放置，如放置在書桌上，它的詞類變化是 set，setting，set 和 set。

    a. Two girls <u>sat</u> on the park bench.

    b. The workers have <u>set</u> their equipment aside.

4. Rise 是動詞，它的意義是起床，為不及物動詞，它的詞類變化為 rise，rising，rose，和 risen。Raise 也是動詞，它的意義是舉起來，為及物動詞，它的詞類變化為 raise，raising，raised 和 raised。

    a. They always <u>rise</u> early on Saturday morning.

    b. The huge crame <u>raises</u> the steel beams off the ground.

5. Lie 是動詞，它的意義是躺著休息，它的詞類變化為 lie，lying，lay 和 lain。lay 也是動詞，它意義為放下，它的詞類變化為 lay，laying，laid 和 laid。

    a. Those dirty clothes have <u>lain</u> in the corner of your room for days.

b. Before the sale, the clerk <u>laid</u> samples on the counter.

c. Finally, the baby is <u>lying</u> quietly in the crib.

d. Yesterday, Father <u>lay</u> down on some hard plastic pieces on the sofa.

6. Good 是形容詞，它的比較級為 better，最高級為 the best，均可為形容詞或代名詞。well 為副詞，它的比較級為 better，最高級為 the best，只能形容形容詞或副詞。

    a. The famers had a <u>good</u> crop this year.

    b. Don't you think the book is <u>better</u> than the movie ?

    c. The day started <u>well</u>.

    d. The football team played <u>better</u> in the second half of the game.

    e. These are <u>the best</u> cultivated fields in this region.

7. Well 的意義如果是表示健康狀態時，就是形容詞。

    a. I'm quite <u>well</u>, thank you.

    b. I hope you'll soon <u>well</u> again.

8. Altogether 是副詞，它的意義是全部地，all together 是形容詞片語，它的意義是每一個人或某物同在一個位置。

    a. There is <u>altogether</u> too much chatting in this study all.

    b. The family is <u>all together</u> at the table.

9. Coarse 是形容詞，它的意義是不純的或不細的，course 是名詞，它的意義是一系列的研究。

    a. The <u>coarse</u> salt can be used to help melt snow on the roadways.

    b. The professor suggested several <u>courses</u> for us to take.

10. Stationary 是形容詞，它的意義是不動的，stationery 是名詞，它的意義是文具用品。

    a. The car was <u>stationary</u> when the accident happened.

    b. The <u>stationery</u> he ordered had a design of shooting stars across the top border.

11. Learn 是動詞，它的意義是需要知識，teach 也是動詞，它的意義是教導。

a. I'm trying to <u>learn</u> French.

b. My wife <u>teaches</u> English at a local school.

12. Than 是連接詞，它的意義是比較，then 是副詞，它的意義是然後。

a. I speak English better <u>than</u> I write.

b. We will eat first, <u>then</u> we will ride our bikes.

13. Be used to 是動詞片語，它的意義是某件事情現在固定的發生。used to 也是動詞片語，它的意義是某件事情在過去常常或有規律的發生，而現在已經停止了。

a. I'<u>m used to</u> getting up at 6:00 in the morning. (現在的習慣)

b. We <u>used to</u> swim every day when we were children. (過去的習慣)

14. Without 是介詞，它的意義是不包括在內，Unless 是連接詞，它的意義是除非。

a. We couldn't have done it <u>without</u> our teacher.

b. I will not be able to go to the party <u>unless</u> I finish my homework first.

15. Loose 是形容詞，它的意義是沒有弄緊，寬鬆的意思，lose 是動詞，它的意義是遭受損失。

a. If a tourniquet is too <u>loose</u>, it will not serve its purpose.

b. Vegetables <u>lose</u> some of their vitamins when they are cooked.

16. Who 是代名詞，被用做述語的主格和主格子句。Whom 被用做述語的受格和受格子句。Whose 被用做述語的所有格，但在附屬子句中常常被省略掉。

a. Rong is the student <u>who</u> got a perfect score.

b. Do you know <u>who</u> the choice was ?

c. The actor (<u>whom</u>) I wrote to sent these photos.

d. The man (<u>whom</u>) we saw on the elevator looked familiar.

17. Some 被用在肯定句中，而 any 被用在否定句和疑問句中。

a. Andy brought <u>some</u> friends to the party.

b. John didn't see <u>any</u> friends in the supermarket.

c. Have you got <u>any</u> matches ?

18. Someone，something，somebody，somewhere，被用在肯定句中。
Anyone，anybody，anything，anywhere 被用在否定句中。

   a. You'd better ask <u>someone</u> to help you.

   b. I heard her whisper <u>something</u> to you.

   c. I didn't see <u>anybody</u> I knew in the room.

   d. I can't find my pen <u>anywhere</u>.

19. Say 被用在直接和間接的引句中，聽者沒有特定的對象。Tell 被用在間接的引句中，但是聽者有特定的對象。

   a. Bill <u>said</u>, "It's too early to leave for the theater."

   b. Henry <u>said</u> that he could not come tomorrow.

   c. Tom <u>told</u> me that his car was at the mechanic's.

20. Still 是一種不確定的時間副詞，它的意義是尚未完成或者甚至到現在還是同樣狀況。它所描述的是一些持續的動作或狀態，如同頻率副詞，still 是放在主動詞之前。still 的否定字是 anymore，它指出動作或狀態已經終止，通常放在句子的結尾。

   a. They <u>still</u> live in the house they were born in.

   b. There are <u>still</u> some tickets left for tonight's show.

   c. He doesn't believe they know him <u>anymore</u>.

   d. We never see you at the school dances <u>anymore</u>.

21. Spill 是非故意的動作，甚至是一種意外，而 pour 是故意的動作。

   a. She carelessly <u>spilled</u> the milk on the floor.

   b. The baby <u>spilled</u> cereal all over the floor.

   c. Mary carefully <u>poured</u> the tea into the cup.

22. Since 表示特定的時間，它是連接詞，副詞和介詞。For 表示時間的量，它是介詞和連接詞。

   a. I've studied English <u>for</u> ten years. (介詞)

   b. My son has studied math <u>since</u> five years ago. (介詞)

   c. He felt no fear, <u>for</u> he was a brave man. (連接詞)

   d. I saw Judy in May and I haven't seen her <u>since</u>. (副詞)

e. Tom hasn't been home <u>since</u> he was a boy. (連接詞)

23. Most 是形容詞，名詞和副詞。Almost 是副詞。

a. The children ate <u>most</u> of the pie. (名詞)

b. The winner gets the <u>most</u> money. (形容詞)

c. He is the one who worked the <u>most</u>, and yet was paid the least. (副詞)

d. The student was <u>almost</u> finished when the bell rang. (副詞)

24. Because 是附屬連接詞，而 because of 是介詞。

a. We could not see anything in the storage <u>because</u> the lighting was poor.

b. He can move the heavy furniture easily <u>because of</u> his strength.

25. Do 和 make 的意義各不相同，要看各種場合而定。

a. I forgot to <u>do</u> my homework last night.

b. My father refuses to <u>do</u> business with dishonest people.

c. She <u>makes</u> the sandwiches for us every morning.

d. He always <u>makes</u> a mistake in the school.

26. Few 是否定的意思，它的意義是不多，a few 是肯定的意思，它的意義是有一些。

a. There were <u>few</u> chairs left, so that I had to stand up.

b. Most people in the United States speak English, but <u>a few</u> speak French.

27. Later 是 late 的比較級，而 latter 是兩個東西或人，同時被指名時的後者。

a. I will see you <u>later</u>.

b. We must all die sooner or <u>later</u>.

c. Of these two men the former is dead and the <u>latter</u> is still alive.

28. Little 的意義是不多，而 a little 的意義是一些，它們均形容不可數的名詞。

a. This computer is easy to operate; you need <u>little</u> skill.

b. Please give me <u>a little</u> more time to finish writing.

29. Already 在否定句中使用並不正常，在肯定句中使用一般都放在句尾。
    yet 在疑問句中和否定句中使用，通常也是放在句尾。

    a. This machine is <u>already</u> out of date.

    b. Tom <u>already</u> knows the truth.

    c. I've seen it <u>already</u>.

    d. Haven't the new petrol prices come into force <u>yet</u> ?

    e. The work is not <u>yet</u> finished.

    f. Can't you tell me <u>yet</u> ?

30. 用介詞片語來介紹方法或手段時是用 by，同樣的，介紹設備或工具時
    是用 with。

    a. The thief must have entered <u>by</u> the back door.

    b. We managed to sell the house <u>by</u> advertising it in the paper.

    c. He caught the ball <u>with</u> his left hand.

    d. Someone killed him <u>with</u> an arrow.

31. Each other 是使用在兩個人時，而三個人或三個人以上時，則使用 one
    another。

    a. The executive and his secretary antagonize <u>each other</u>.

    b. The members of the large family love <u>one another</u>.

32. Accept 是動詞，它的意義是接受，except 是動詞也是介詞，當動詞時
    意義為忽略或遺漏，當介詞時意義為排除在外。

    a. I <u>accept</u> your apology.

    b. Some students will be <u>excepted</u> from this assignment.

    c. Mark has written all his friends <u>except</u> John.

33. Affect 是動詞，它的意義是影響，effect 是動詞也是名詞，當動詞時的
    意義為完成，當名詞時的意義為某些行動的結果。

    a. His score on this test will <u>affect</u> his final grade.

    b. Bo and Alice's hard work <u>effected</u> a solution to the problem.

    c. The <u>effects</u> of the medicine were immediate.

34. All right 是兩個字，不可合併寫成 allright，可當形容詞和副詞。

a. Your work is <u>all right</u>. (形容詞)

b. Maria fell, but she is <u>all right</u>. (形容詞)

c. You did <u>all right</u> at the track meet. (副詞)

35. Between 和 Among 均為介詞，但 between 是使用在兩個人（或物）之間，而 among 則使用在三個人（或物）之間。

a. In English, Marc sits <u>between</u> Bob and me.

b. Some players practice <u>between</u> innings.

c. Next year we will study the War <u>between</u> the States.

d. There was disagreement <u>among</u> the players about the coach's decision.

e. We saved twenty dollars <u>among</u> the three of us.

36. your 是 you 的所有格，而 you're 是 you are 的縮寫。

a. <u>Your</u> dinner is on the table.

b. <u>You're</u> one of my closest friends.

37. Beside 是介詞，它的意義是在某個人或某個物的旁邊。Besides 是介詞也是副詞，當介詞時的意義為除此之外還附加；當副詞時的意義為而且或此外。

a. Sit <u>beside</u> me on the couch.

b. <u>Besides</u> songs and dances, the show featured several comedy sketches.

c. I have a long walk home. <u>Besides</u>, it's starting to snow.

38. Bring 和 take 均為動詞，但是 bring 是帶著某種東西來，而 take 是拿著某種東西走。

a. <u>Bring</u> that box over here.

b. Now <u>take</u> it down to the basement.

39. Discover 和 invent 均為動詞，但是 discover 的意義是首先發現，看見或學習的某件事物，而那件事物已經存在。至於 invent 的意義是首先做或製造某件事物。

a. Marguerite Perey <u>discovered</u> the element francium.

b. The zipper was <u>invented</u> in 1925.

40. Like 是介詞，在非正式的英文中，往往被用做連接詞來代替 as。其實在正式的英文裡，as 當連接詞是較適合的。

　　a. She looks <u>like</u> her sister. (介詞片語)

　　b. We should do <u>as</u> our coach recommends. (子句)

41. Allusion 和 illusion 均為名詞，但是它們的意義卻大不相同。allusion 的意義為引述某件事物，而 illusion 的意義為錯覺。

　　a. She made an <u>allusion</u> to the poem.

　　b. The magician was a master of <u>illusion</u>.

42. Imply 和 infer 均為動詞，imply 的意義為暗示，而 infer 的意義為推論。

　　a. In her speech, the candidate <u>implied</u> that she was for tax reform.

　　b. From other remarks that she has made, I <u>infer</u> that she feels that certain taxes are unfair.

43. Respectfully 和 respectively 均為副詞，雖然發音相似，它們的意義卻完全不同。respectfully 的意義為完全尊重地，而 respectively 的意義為個別依序地。

　　a. The reporters listened <u>respectfully</u> to the sentator's request.

　　b. Nick, Margo, and Ted are nineteen, seventeen, and fifteen, <u>respectively</u>.

44. Alumni 是 alumnae 的複數，指的是男校友，alumnae 是 alumna 的複數，指的是女校友。

　　a. All my sisters are <u>alumnae</u> of Adams High School.

　　b. Both men are <u>alumni</u> of Haward.

　　c. My parents went to their college <u>alumni</u> reunion.

45. Amount，the number of 和 a number of 三者的區別，amount 和 the number of 使用單數動詞，而 a number of 與複數字有關，因此要使用複數動詞。

　　a. <u>The amount of</u> research (單數) on stress is overwhelming.

b. <u>A number of</u> reports (複數) on stress are available.

c. <u>The number of</u> candidates was surprising.

d. <u>A number of</u> candidates were nominated by the committee.

46. And 和 etc.因為 etc.是拉丁字 et cetera 的簡寫，它的意義是其它的人或事物。如果寫成 and etc.就變成 and 重複使用。

a. The new store in the mall sells videotapes, audio, cassettes, cameras, radios, electronic games, <u>etc.</u>

b. Our courses are English, Chinese, European History, computer, writing, <u>etc.</u>

47. Credible，creditable 和 credulous 三者長得太像了，但是它們的意義卻完全不同。credible 的意義是可相信的，creditable 的意義是值得稱讚的，而 credulous 的意義是輕信的。

a. The child gave a <u>credible</u> excuse for breaking the window in the kitchen.

b. Her quick thinking and competent action were <u>creditable</u>.

c. The <u>credulous</u> woman and her neighbors signed up for the trip to Mars.

48. Emigrate 的意義是移出到別的國家，而 immigrate 的意義是移入到一個國家。

a. The war has forced thousands of people to <u>emigrate</u> from their homeland to other, more peaceful countries.

b. Marie's grandparents <u>immigrated</u> here in 1950.

49. Data 是拉丁字 datum 的複數，在標準正式的英文裡，data 永遠是複數用複數動詞。不過在非正式的英文中，往往被誤用。

a. The census <u>data</u> <u>was</u> finally published. (非正式)

b. The census <u>data</u> <u>were</u> finally published. (正式)

50. In 的意義是在裡面，它是靜態的；而 into 的意義是往裡面，它是動態的。

a. Feeling nervous, I walked <u>into</u> the personnel office. (不是用 in)

b. We threw some pennies <u>into</u> the well and made a wish. (不是用 in)

c. Her cousin will teach <u>in</u> San Diego next year. (不是用 into)

d. There are 100 people <u>in</u> the dormitory. (不是用 into)

51. Persecute 的意義是迫害，而 prosecute 的意是控告。

a. The old regime <u>persecuted</u> those who held opposing views.

b. The district attorney will <u>prosecute</u> anyone caught looting.

第十四章 │ 標點符號和簡寫（Punctuations & Contractions）

1. 我們都知道標點符號的重要性，大家都應該還記得小學老師都會講一個有關標點符號，放在不同位置而造成的笑話。請看下列兩則，由於標點符號和所放位置的不同，它們的意義卻完全走了樣。因此，我們不但要使用正確的標點符號，而且要放在正確的位置。

※下雨天，留客天，天留，我不留。

※下雨天，留客天，天留我不？留。

2. 劃底線（或斜體字）＿＿＿＿或////////。

書名，定期刊物，藝術作品，船舶，影片和電視節目等。

   a. The Island Princess is a cruise ship.

   b. The <u>Island Princess</u> is a cruise ship.

   c. I saw some good article in Time and Newsweek.

   d. I saw some good article in <u>Time and Newsweek</u>.

3. 雙引號—— " "

直接引用別人所說或所寫的字語。

A. 直接引用時，第一個字母要大寫。

   a. Mrs. Talbott said, "Please get a pencil."

   b. Karistina asked, "Is it my turn ?"

B. 直接引用時，如被插話，表達分成兩個部分的時候要用小寫。

   * "Could you take care of my lawn," asked Mr. Franklin, "while I'm on vocation next month ?"

不過，假如第二個部分是被打破的引用，而另外成新的句子時，要用大寫。

　　　　* "I don't know, " I said. "My mother wants me to practice the piano
　　　　　more".

4.　句號——　.
　　只要一個完整的句子，最後句尾一定要加上句號，做為結束陳述。

　　　　a. The lens is the most important part of a camera.

　　　　b. One of the figure skaters was Sonja Henie.

5.　疑問號——　?
　　疑問句的句尾要加上問號，尋求別人的答案。

　　　　a. Have you watched Barbara Walters ?

　　　　b. Is photograpy a science or an art ?

6.　點號——　,
　　點號與句號不同，它不是句子的完全結束，而是表示一段落。如果能
　　夠充分的使用點號，將字、片語和子句加以分開，可以讓整個句子更
　　加清晰，而讀者唸起來會一目了然。

　　A.　將一系列的字分開

　　　　a. We have read poems by Longfellow, Teasdale, and Dickinson this
　　　　　week.

　　　　b. Tobacco, hammock, canoe, and moccasin are four of the words that
　　　　　English-speaking people owe to American Indians.

　　　　c. In the early morning, the lake looked cold, gray, and uninviting.

　　　　d. 有些作者習慣將 and 連接前的點號省略，因而造成困擾。

　　　　　* Susie, Zack and I are going riding. (不清晰)

　　　　　* Susie, Zack, and I are going riding. (清晰有 3 個人)

　　B.　將一系列的片語分開

　　　　a. We found seaweed in the water, on the sand, under the rocks, and even
　　　　　in our shoes.

　　　　b. It makes no difference whether that hamster is in a cage, on a string,
　　　　　or under a net-it always escapes.

　　C.　將附屬子句和主要子句分開。

a. Everyone wondered when he had been in the house, what he had wanted and where he had gone.

b. We worked, we played, and we rested.

7. 假如所有的項目在一系列用 and 或者 or 連結時，不可使用點號將它們分開。

* Have you read Huckleberry Finn or Tom Sawyer or A Connecticut Yankee in King Arthur's Court ?

8. 使用點號將名詞前一個或兩個以上的形容詞分開。

a. An Arabian horse is a fast, beautiful animal.

b. The rancher of old often depended on the small, tough, sure-footed mustang.

9. 當最後一個形容詞和名詞的關係非常緊密，可以認為是一個表述時，不可加上點號將它們分開。

* Training a frisky colt to become a gentle, dependable riding horse takes great patience.

（riding horse 連在一起）

10. 最後一個形容詞緊接著是名詞時，不可加上點號將它們分開。

* Mary O'Hara wrote a tender, suspenseful, story about a young boy and his colt. (不正確)

* Mary O'Hara wrote a tender, suspenseful story about a young boy and his colt. (正確)

11. 在一些句子裡，分詞片語和形容詞片語是主要思想，除非毀壞句子的意義，否則不能移除。在此情況下，不能加上點號，將分詞片語或形容詞片語和它們所要形容的字分開。

a. All farmers growing hybrid corn owe a debt to an Austrian monk named Gregor Mendel.

b. Mendel made the discoveries that have become the basis of modern genetice.

c. Anyone who finishes early may start on tomorrow's assignment.

12. 假如分詞片語或形容詞片語並不是句子中的主要思想，那麼將它們移除也不會改變整個句子的原來意義時，就要用點號將它們分開。

    a. Sometimes seeds and nuts, forgotten by the squirrels that hid them, germinate far away from their parent plants.

    b. Migrating birds, which often fly hundres of thousands of miles, are one of the main carries of seeds.

    c. A new spider web, shining in the morning light, is an impressive example of engineering.

13. 假如用分詞片語或者副詞子句當句子的起頭時，必須要用點號，因為它們負責引導整個句子。不過，副詞子句如果放在句尾就不需要加點號。

    a. Forced onto the sidelines by a torn ligament, Harris was restless and unhappy.

    b. When March came, the huge ice pack began to melt and break up.

    c. The huge ice pack began to melt and break up when March came.

14. 當一個表達詞，如 of course，well 或 why 等等，或一個人的名字中斷句子時，點號是必需的。如果這個中斷的狀況放在句首或句尾時，只有一個點號是需要的。如果中斷發出在句子的中間時，如同位字或同位片語，兩個點號是必需的。

    a. Why, you really should know that.

    b. Well, I don't.

    c. My best friend, Nancy, is studying ballet.

    d. We're out of our most popular flavor, vanilla.

    e. Nancy, my best friend, has won a dance scholarship.

    f. The Rio Grande, one of the major rivers of North America, forms that of the border between Texas and Mexico.

15. 如果同位字很短，而且與其跟隨的名詞關係非常密切，此時不需要使用點號。

    a. My ancestor Alberto Pazienza emigrated to America on the ship

Marianna.

    b. White House spokesman Larry Speaks issued a statement.

16. 當某一個人直接向另一個說話，此時該人的名字之外，需要使用點號。

    a. Mrs. Clarkson, I just want to get to the beach.

    b. Can you tell me, Hagel, when the next bus is due?

17. 通常一個句子中，有插句的時候，如 tell the truth，in my opinion，in fact 等等，就好像字放在括弧內，因為它們與句子的文法無關，此時點號是必需的。

    a. The President said, off the record, that he was deeply disappointed.

    b. To be honest, I thought the movie was fairly good.

    c. It wasn't very good, in my opinion.

18. 並不是所有的陳述詞都認為是插句，因此要很小心的使用點號，真正需要的時候才要用上。

    a. What, in her opinion, is the best closing hour?(插句)

    b. I have no faith in her opinion.(非插句)

    c. Traveling by boat may take longer, However.(插句)

    d. However you go, it will be a delightful trip.(非插句)

19. 日期，地址，信的起頭稱謂和結尾均需使用點號。

    a. The delegates to the Constitutional Convention signed the Constitution on September 17, 1787, in Philadelphia Pennsylvania.

    b. Passover begins on Wednesday, April 14, this year.

    c. My friend has just moved to 6358 Higgins Road, Chicago Illinois.

    d. Jackson Heights, New York 11372

    e. Dear Aunt Margaret,

    f. Sincerely yours,

    g. Yours truly,

20. 句號，點號，疑問號，或驚嘆號必須放在引號裡面。

    a. "I can't wait to go tubing," I said excitedly.

b Jim added, "It should be lots of fun."

c. "Are we almost there, Dad ?" asked Charles.

d. "This water is freezing !"

21. 如果引號用的句子不是疑問句，也不是驚嘆句時，疑問號或驚嘆號要放在引號的外面。不過，整個句子仍然當做疑問句或驚嘆句。

a. Who said, "Let's go tubing on Saturday" ?

b. What a shock to hear Barbara say, "I think I'll sit down and watch the rest of you" !

22. 分號—— ;

在一個句子中，停止的訊號，分號比點號強一些，但又比句號弱一點點。

a. On our first trip to Houton I wanted to see the Astrodome; my little brother wanted to visit the Johnson Space Center. (兩個附屬子句之間)

b. Our parents settled the argument for us; they took us to see a rodeo in a nearby town. (兩個附屬子句之間)

c. Mary Ishikawa decided not to stay at home; instead, she went to the game. (兩個附屬子句之間，但有中斷語詞)

d. The popular names of certain animak are misleading; for example, the koala bear is not a bear. (兩個附屬子句之間，但有中斷語詞)

e. English was Louise's difficult subject; accordingly, she gave it more time than any other subject. (兩個附屬子句之間，但有中斷語詞)

23. 如果附屬子句很短，而且沒有連接詞時，可以用點號加以分開。

* The leaves whispered, the brook gurgled, the sun beamed benignly.

24. 在複合句中的附屬子句之間，一而再，再而三的使用點號加以分開它們，會造成困擾，此時分號的使用是必需的。

* A tall, slender woman entered the large, drafty room; and a short, slight, blond woman followed her.

25. 冒號—— :

在一系列的項目中要表達，或者特殊的習慣場合使用。

    a. Minimum equipment for camping is as follows: bedroll, untensils for cooking and eating, warm clothing, sturdy shoes, jackknife, rope, and flashlight.

    b. This is what I have to do: clean my room, shop for a birthday present, baby-sit for Mrs. Magill for two hours, and do my Spanish homework.

    c. 11:30 P.M.

    d. 5:08 A.M.

    e. Gentlemen:

    f. Dear Sir:

26. 省略符號——'

在表示所有者或關係者之外，同時表示那些省略的字母，在簡寫時使用。

    a. An hour's time

    b. a book's title

    c. Mother's job

    d. a dog's collar

    e. one cent's worth

    f. Hercules' feats

    g. pupils' records

    h. women's group

    i. Where's the exit ?

    j. We'll have gone by then.

    k. You're going to get a better mark this term.

    l. It's been a long time.

27. 省略符號加上 s 或構成字母，數字，和招牌等等的複數型態。

    a. Doesn't he know the ABC's ?

    b. Your 2's look like 5's.

    c. Don't use &'s in place of and's.

d. I hope to make all A's.

28. 連字號（一個字母的長度）── -

在寫作時如果碰到紙張無法全部容納一個字時，此時被迫不得不使用連字號，將一個字的全部字母從上一行到下一行，或上一頁到下一頁連接起來。不過要注意的是要以母音將字分成兩半，不可隨意自行分開，同時單字母或單音節不可分開。

a. How long has the building been under con-struction.

b. If you want to know, look it up in the al-manac.

c. Uncle Steve, Aunt Sue, and Kendra will jou-rney eighty miles to join us. (不可)

Uncle Steve, Aunt Sue, and Kendra will jour-ney eighty miles to join us. (可以)

d. They are bringing salad, ham, and rye bre-ad. (不可)

They are bringing salad, ham and rye bread. (可以)

e. I understand that the family car is parked a-cross the street. (不可)

I understand that the family car is parked across the street. (可以)

29. 複合數字通常以連字號連接，從 21 到 99 當做形容詞。

a. There were twenty-one ducks in that flock.

b. A two-thirds majority will decide the issue, and the other one-third will have to abide by the decision.

30. 破折號（又稱長劃符號）── ──

在寫作時，表示思想的突然破裂或者在陳述前有指明，換句話說，那就是等著意念在內時使用。

a. He might ── if I have anything to say about it ── change this mind.

b. The truth is ── and you probably know it ── we can't do it without you.

c. It was a close call ── the sudden gust of wind pushed the helicopter to within inches of the power line.

31. 冒號和破折號經常可以交換使用。

     * It was a close call: the sudden gust of wind pushed the helicopter to within inches of the power line.

32. 括號——（　）

使用括號是將附帶的說明事項，在句子中是屬於附加的，而且被認為不是主要的。

    a. Former Representative Jordan (Texas) was on that committee.

    b. The population of the United States is shifting (see Chart B) to the South and the Southwest.

    c. Fred Bates asked us (What a silly question !) if we really thought we could do it.

    d. If the committee is headed by Alison (Is she here ?), the student council will probably support it.

33. 括弧——[　]

括弧並不常用，當附帶的說明事項並不在引用的範圍內時使用。

    a. Ms. Gray was quoted as saying in her acceptance speech: "I am honored by it [the award], but I would like to share the recognition with those who make my work possible."

    b. By vote 5-4, the Supreme Court overturned the lower court's ruling. (See page 149 [Diagram A] for a chronology of the case.)

34. 單引號——‘’

直接引用別人的說話，而說話者又特別提出書名，簡短故事，詩，歌曲等等時，大範圍事項用雙引號，小範圍事項則用單引號，也就是雙引號在外，單引號在內。

    a. "Tonight you must read the Chapter 'Comets and Asteroids,' " stated Mr. Mendoza.

    b. "Mrs. Engle distinctly said, 'your book reports are due Thursday,' " Krista told me.

第十五章 | # 練習題（Practices）

1. The employee entered the correct code and the gate (rose/rise).

2. If we had (known/knew) how long the movie was, we wouldn't have rented it.

3. The children always have (laid/lain) the money on the counter when they arrived, but today it was not there.

4. I bought new running shoes because the heels had (worn/wore) down in the old ones.

5. The laundry had (shrunk/shrinked) my only good shirt just before the awards dinner.

6. My sister and I used to get along (badly/bad).

7. She said that I played my radio too (loudly/loud).

8. Now we get along (well/good).

9. While I'm thinking of my sister, I will call her (quickly/quick) on the phone.

10. We were always (ready/readily) to fight.

11. I said that she did not behave (politely/polite) toward me.

12. Since I'm never at fault, it must be that she is acting (immaturely/immature).

13. Jose will call (immediately/immediate) after he arrives.

14. The chorus sings (well/good).

15. My nine year old son runs (quickly/quick).

16. The old dog walked (lazily/lazy) down the street.

17. A (quick/quickly) call will tell me everything I need to know.

18. An abject Terry apologized (sincerely/sincere).

19. A good singer breathes (deeply/deep).

20. Did you ever have a neighbor who loved (loud/loudly) music.

21. The authors say, "Study each chapter (carefully/careful)."

22. The software works (well/good) for this project.

23. Each (gives/give) a lecture.

24. They each (give/gives) a lecture.

25. Each of the teachers (gives/give) a lecture.

26. Each (is/are) a good candidate.

27. (Whom/Who) did you call ?

28. (Who/Whom) will help with this project ?

29. Mariah Carey is the singer (whom/who) Tony likes best.

30. (Who/Whom) answered your letter ?

31. Consumer Reports cites manufacturers from (whom/who) we can expect quality products.

32. Mr. Jones and (he/him) ran the fair.

33. My friend and (I/me) are planning a camping trip.

34. The Walters and (we/us) go to the shore each summer.

35. (They/Them) and their father went fishing.

36. (She/Her) and (he/him) were delegates to the convention.

37. (Who/Whom), along with Susan, will work on this committee ?

38. My secretary is (she/her).

39. (Who/Whom) seems most likely to get the promotion ?

40. The person who called you was (I/me).

41. Tom is very proud of (his/him) swimming.

42. The professor was glad to hear about (my/me) writing a story.

43. I don't like (their/them) refusing to take BHA and BHT out of foods.

44. I don't like (your/you) calling me at the office.

45. We wondered (whose/who's) contribution to medicine was greast.

46. From (whom/who) did you learn that myth about not eating before swimming ?

47. The personnel director gave notices to John and (them/they).

48. The host and his friends divided the four bottles of beer among (them/they).

49. Many secrets have passed between you and (him/he).

50. Everyone, except (her/she), plans to take the test.

51. Everyone must decide for (himself/themselves).

52. They each performed to the best of (their/his) ability.

53. Each of the painters worked (his/their) best.

54. All of the members brought (their/his) wives.

55. Every (July/july), my cousin visit us.

56. Mr. Lieu (raised/rased) money for the Heart Association.

57. Ben moved to (Los Angeles, California/Los Angeles California).

58. We (tried/tired) to finish on time.

59. French, Spanish, and (Latin/latin) are taught at our school.

60. Ryan and Kelly played (checkers. Kelly/checkers Kelly) won.

61. Heather's team won the baseball (game./game)

62. We bought (two/too) tickets to the game.

63. Bob and Jane came (in/on) on the train.

64. Gold has many (uses/usages).

65. Please help me find my (umbrella./umbrella)

66. Have you been to a video (store ?/store)

67. My father and I are cleaning the (attic./attic)

68. We toured the government (district./district)

69. My surprise visit pleased my (grandmother./grandmother)

70. How happy I (am !/am)

71. Go east for three blocks and look for a (mailbox./mailbox)

72. What a delicious ham this (is !/is.)

73. Do you like charcoal-grilled (hamburgers ?/hamburgers.)

74. When is your next piano (lesson ?/lesson !)

75. The flowers in that garden (need/needs) water.

76. Neither the tomatoes nor the peach (is/are) ripe.

77. My brother and his dog (have/has) gone hunting.

78. It (doesn't/don't) really matter to me.

79. (Were/Was) they invited to the party ?

80. She and her cousin (play/plays) tennis every weekend.

81. There (were/was) several teachers at the game.

82. (Were/Was) your friends at the concert last Saturday ?

83. My friends at school (don't/doesn't) live in our district.

84. Here (come/comes) Elena and James.

85. The second largest island of the United States (is/are) located in the Gulf of Alaska.

86. Sacks of mail (are/is) flown to the island from the mainland.

87. Industries in the community (have/has) suffered in recent years.

88. The residents of the mainland (consider/considers) roe a delicacy.

89. However, their search for leftovers (creates/create) problems for Kodiak.

90. The 13,000 citizens on Kodia Island (are/is) of Eskimo, Russian, or Scandinavian descent.

91. The citizens of Kodiak (call/calls) Alaska the mainland.

92. One cannery on the island (cans/can) delicious salmon eggs, or roe.

93. The bears on the island (catch/catches) fresh salmon.

94. The officials of one town (have/has) put a special fence around the garbage dump.

95. A train and a truck (have/has) powerful engines.

96. A desk and a bookcase (were/was) moved into my younger brother's bedroom.

97. A car and a trailer (were/was) stalled on the highway.

98. Ms. Wilson and her niece (go/goes) to class together.

99. Mosquitoes and earwigs (have/has) invaded our back yard.

100. Wind and rain (are/is) predicted for Thursday.

101. Savannas and velds (are/is) two kinds of grasslands.

102. A raccoon and a squirrel (raid/raids) our garden every night.

103. Joan and Jarvis (were/was) asked to introduce the guest speaker.

104. Catsup and mustard (go/goes) well on hot dogs.

105. Some house plants (bloom/blooms) all winter.

106. The sailboats in the harbor (belong/belongs) to the village.

107. Either the clock or our watches (are/is) not accurate.

108. A stretch of unpaved roads (lies/lie) ahead.

109. Neither pencils nor an eraser (is/are) permitted.

110. His mother (teaches/teach) math.

111. You and your cousin (are/is) invited to the party.

112. The magazines on the table (are/is) for the hospital.

113. My brother and sister (deliver/delivers) newspapers.

114. Stories by that writer (have/has) unexpected endings.

115. Mrs. Shea or her father (sweeps/sweep) their front path every day.

116. Heavy rains in the spring (have/has) swollen the rivers.

117. My sister or my parents (have/has) promised us a ride.

118. Sherbet or fresh fruit (makes/make) a tasty dessert.

119. Wind and rain (are/is) forecast for Thanksgiving.

120. My blouse and skirt (were/was) birthday gifts from my Dad.

121. The fate of the players (depends/depend) on the coach's instruction.

122. Neither the chief nor the deouties (need/needs) a new car.

123. The windows in my room (are/is) stuck.

124. There (are/is) three foreign exchange students at the high school.

125. (Have/Has) the Washingtons moved into their new home ?

126. (Have/Has) the bees left the hive ?

127. (Have/Has) the sixth-graders elected their officers ?

128. (There's/There are) a pint of strawberries in the kitchen.

129. There (are/is) Amy and Wanda in the doorway.

130. (Were/Was) the fans cheering for the other team ?

131. Here (is/are) my copy of the words to the song.

132. (There are/There's) several answers to that question.

133. (Here are/Here's) the shells from Driftwood Beach.

134. Neither the passengers nor the pilot (was/were) injured.

135. The stuffed animals in my collection (sit/sits) on a shelf in my closet.

136. Shel Silverstein and Ogden Nash (appeal/appeals) to children and grownups.

137. (Were/Was) your parents happy with the results ?

138. He (doesn't/don't) play chess anymore.

139. There (are/is) two new rides at the amusement park.

140. (Here are/Here's) some books about Hawaii.

141. My neighbor and his son (are/is) building a log cabin.

142. Why (don't/doesn't) she and Megan bring the lemonade ?

143. The dishes on the shelf (look/looks) clean.

144. Either the cats or the dog (has/have) upset the plants.

145. There (go/goes) Jane and her brother.

146. Why (weren't/wasn't) you at the meeting yesterday ?

147. Several paintings by that artist (are/is) on exhibit at the mall.

148. Tickets for that concert (are/is) scarce.

149. My mother and my brother (have/has) been in Florida since Sunday.

150. Here (are/is) the instructions for the microwave.

151. I (am/is) crocheting an afghan.

152. She (doesn't/don't) like spectator sports.

153. They (don't/doesn't) know the correct time.

154. Earline has never (drunk/drank) buttermilk before.

155. Before the lecture, I had never (known/knew) the difference between cricket and croquet.

156. Who (swam/swum) faster, Jesse or Cindy ?

157. We (did/done) our homework after dinner.

158. The lake has finally (frozen/froze) hard enough for us to go skating on it.

159. That cute little puppy has (stolen/stole) our hearts.

160. Anna and Dee have almost (broken/broke) the school record for the fifty-yard dash.

161. My father has (given/gave) away all my comic books to the children's hospital.

162. The choir has never (sung/sang) beautifully.

163. The wind has (blown/blew) fiercely for three days.

164. The school bell (rang/rung) five minutes late every afternoon this week.

165. Jimmy's toy boat (sank/sunk) to the bottom of the lake where we could not see it.

166. Last Saturday, Isaac and Charles (came/come) to my house for the afternoon.

167. In New York, Julia (saw/seen) a musical about cats.

168. Have you (thrown/throwed) away yesterday's paper ?

169. The hot-water pipes in the laundry room have (burst/bursted) again.

170. How many sixth-graders have never (ridden/rode) on the school bus ?

171. Maria had (worn/wore) her new outfit to the party.

172. We had (begun/began) our project when I got sick.

173. It is amazing that no one has ever (fallen/fell) off the old ladder.

174. Until yesterday, no one had ever (swum/swam) across Crystal Lake.

175. The Ruiz family has (driven/drove) across the country.

176. What is the longest distance you have ever (run/ran) ?

177. In Alice's Adventures in Wonderland, Alice (shrank/shrunk) to a very small size !

178. Has anyone (brought/brung) extra batteries for the radio ?

179. Everyone has (gone/went) back to the classroom to watch the Videotape of the spelling bee.

180. The students have (written/wrote) a letter to the mayor.

181. I have finally (chosen/chose) the orange kitten.

182. George (ran/run) to the corner to see the antique fire engine.

183. I have never (spoken/spoke) to a large group before.

184. For many years, the trunk had (sat/set) in the attic.

185. Never (set/sit) your roller skates on the stairs.

186. Where has Chester (laid/lain) the jigsaw puzzle ?

187. Mom has (lain/laid) down for a nap.

188. The magician (raised/rose) the wand to make the dove disappear.

189. Yesterday, Barbara (lay/laid) in bed until noon.

190. Marvel (sits/sets) in his favorite chair to watch hockey.

191. The rocket is (rising/raising) into the sky.

192. After the first jump, the official (raises/rises) the bar two inches higher.

193. Under the starry sky, the campers were (lying/laying) in their sleeping bags.

194. (He/Him) and I thought the myth was funny.

195. Neither (she/her) nor Doreen wanted to play a statue that came to life.

196. (He/Him) and I flipped a coin to see who would play the part of Pygmalion.

197. Doreen and (I/me) giggled when Brad pretended to make the beautiful statue.

198. In the skit, when Pygmalion returned from the festival of Venus, (he/him) and the statue were supposed to hug.

199. (We/Us) actors finally look a bow, and the class applauded.

200. Was that (he/him) at the door ?

201. Mr. O'Connor said that the next ones are (they/them).

202. Every year the speaker has been (she/her).

203. The football fans in the family are Dad and (she/her).

204. It might have been (he/him).

205. The winners are you and (I/me).

206. Could it have been (we/us) ?

207. That was Carl and (they/them) in the swimming pool.

208. Last on the program will be (we/us).

209. It was (he/him).

210. Last night, Jennifer and (I/me) went to the library.

211. Were (he/him) and (she/her) in the horse costume ?

212. The candidates for club secretary were Aretha and (I/me).

213. This year (we/us) students can try out for the band.

214. It was not (we/us) players who started the argument.

215. Mr. Kowalski and (he/him) were the judges.

216. That was (they/them) on television.

217. At the party, were (she/her) and (they/them) singing songs ?

218. Could the last runners be (they/them) ?

219. It might have been (I/me) near the drinking fountain.

220. Ms. Jewel, our kindergarten teacher, recognized (us/we) girls at the shopping mall.

221. The store clerk gave (them/they) a discount.

222. The shoes don't fit either (her/she) or (me/I).

223. Would someone please hand (me/I) a towel ?

224. Somebody asked (us/we) girls for the time.

225. The nice waiter brought (us/we) some ice water.

226. The puppy followed Louis and (him/he) all the way home.

227. Have they made (me/I) a program of the recital.

228. Odessa thanked (her/she) and (me/I) for helping.

229. The volunteers showed (us/we) and (them/they) a movie.

230. The spectators watched (us/we) and (them/they).

231. We sewed (him/he) and (her/she) matching book bags.

232. Sean called Marco and (him/he) on the telephone.

233. Those green apples gave Earl and (him/he) stomachaches.

234. The neighbors hired Tia and (us/we) to rake their yard.

235. Why don't you sing (her/she) a lullaby ?

236. Ice water tastes (good/well) on a hot day.

237. Which one is (taller/tallest), Mark or Jim ?

238. Sergio always plays (well/good) during an important game.

239. They could see the eclipse (more clearly/more clear) than we could.

240. Of all the days in the week, Friday goes by (most slowly/more slowly).

241. This is the (darkest/darker) of the three copies.

242. Mr. Smith advised me to be (more attentive/most attentive) than I had been in yesterday's rehearsal.

243. Some people think that the flight of Voyager is the (most amazing/amazingest) of all the space flights.

244. The wind howled (fiercely/fierce) last night.

245. The canned goods make my backpack the (heaviest/heavier) of all the backpacks.

246. The basset hound is the (saddest/most sad) looking dog on the block.

247. Which of the two coats will be (warmer/warmest) ?

248. Ernest didn't feel (good/well) about losing the game.

249. I feel (better/more better) today.

250. That was the (funniest/most funniest) joke we ever heard.

251. Rodney hardly said (anything/nothing).

252. Sheila didn't tell (anyone/no one) about her grade.

253. Mark Twain probably wouldn't care (anything/nothing) about riding in cars and buses.

254. She says she (never/doesn't never) shows her diary to anyone.

255. To Odelle, skipping a day seems (worse/worser) than having the measles.

256. Our (spring/Spring) break begins on March 26.

257. In 1979 the Nobel (Prize/prize) for Peace was given to Mother Teresa.

258. The last day of school is (June/june) 5.

259. Are you going to sign up for (art/Art) next session ?

260. We could see (Mount/mount) hood from the airplane window.

261. It will take for (Africa/africa) to recover from the drought.

262. What plans have you made for (Mother's/mother's) Day ?

263. Our baby brother was born at (Memorial/memorial) Hospital.

264. Congress is composed of the (Senate/senate) and the (House/house) of (Representatives/representatives).

265. Will you see any fireworks on the (Fourth/fourth) of July ?

266. During the class trip, I walked all the way up the Washington (Monument/monument).

267. There is a detour on (Highway/highway) 55.

268. Our first camping trip is planned for (October/october), when the weather is brisk.

269. At the graduation exercises, (Judge/judge) Tucker congratulated the graduates and their parents.

270. Write to (Senator Smith/senator smith) about the new issues.

271. I would love to go on a raft trip down the Colorado (River/river).

272. I would like a book about World (War/war) II.

27. Just after 3:00 (P.M./PM) the sun came out.

274. What traffic there was on First Avenue (!/?)

275. Today is (sunny and/sunny, and) warm.

276. My transportation is a rusty, (ancient bicycle/ancient, bicycle).

277. The (stately pine/stately, pine) tree shook in the wind.

278. Uncle Lee, Aunt Sue, and Kendra will (jour-ney/jou-rney) eighty miles to join us.

279. They are bringing salad, ham, and (rye bread/rye bre-ad).

280. I understand that the family car is parked (across/a-cross) the street.

281. The counselor suggested several (courses/coarses) for us to take.

282. Although the ship was sinking, the loyal crew would not (desert/dessert) the captain.

283. It took over a (week/weak) to complete the project in health class.

284. Which of these (two/to/too) boxes of (stationery/stationary) do you like better ?

285. The (principal/principle) raised his arms for silence, and the students grew quite to (hear/here) what he would say.

286. Mr. Allen praised (Tom, who/Tom who) had written an excellent paper.

287. Mr. Brown gave a slide (show , which/show which) the entire class enjoyed.

288. Frank played his favorite (record, which/record which) I had given to him.

289. This is my favorite (coin, which/coin which) I bought four years ago.

290. This is the (coin that/coin, that) I told you about.

291. Casals began to play, and the crowd was awed by the strength of (her/she) serve.

292. I remembered that Casals had won (my/me) admiration by fighting for equal rights for women in professional tennis.

293. Several people in the audience showed by (their/them) enthusiasm that they had enjoyed watching the matches.

294. The snowstorm has (completely/complete) blocked traffic and has temporarily grounded airplanes today.

295. The coach argued (violently/violent), but the umpire (calmly/calm) ignored him.

296. Today astronomers can (accurately/accurate) chart the courses of planets, yet the motions of some celestial bodies are still mystery.

297. (According to/Due to) legend, Mars was the father of Romulus and Remus, twin brothers.

298. When the twins were babies, an evil ruler threw them (into/in) the Tiber River.

299. Everyone (except/of) the captain can hear the rejoicing.

300. The disc jockey played records (and/which) tapes for us.

301. We were afraid that (neither/either) the Ferris wheel nor the roller coaster was safe.

302. The girl's basketball team not only won the game (but also/and) scored the most points in our school's history.

303. I hope I improve my grades, (for/to) I have been studying hard this term.

304. I didn't receive a letter from my cousin today, (nor/or) did I really expect one.

305. The people waited patiently for the bus, (but/that) it never came.

306. The principal was excited, (for/and) the school board had approved his plan for a new cafeteria.

307. The colonel will be commending the scout for (volunteering/volunteer) for the dangerous mission.

308. (Shouting/Shout) at people does not make them understand you better.

309. Most of the players obeyed the stern (warning/warn) from the coach.

310. The vultures didn't let anything disturb (their/them) feeding.

311. The frantic (darting/dart) of the fish indicated that a shark was nearby.

312. Sometimes I get up (to move/moving) with the music, but June never does.

313. After doing my best (to teach/teaching) her for three weeks, I gave up.

314. It's a good thing that June doesn't plan (to become/becoming) a dancer.

315. No medicine could save the sailors, (who died/whom died) quickly and painfully.

316. Even doctors caught the illness (when/what) they hurried to the besides of sick patients.

317. (Since medicine/Medicine) offers new ways for controlling plague, the spread of this disease is unlikely today.

318. A black hole, (which/that) results after a star has collapsed, can trap energy and matter.

319. Helen Keller was a remarkable woman (who/whom) overcame blindness and deafness.

320. The ones (whose/who) flight was delayed spent the night in Detroit.

321. A special award was given to the student (whose/who) work had improved most.

322. The astronauts, (to whom/who) travel in the space shuttle is routine, must always keep in shap.

323. (After/That) we spent three hours in the theater, the movie finally ended.

324. (Whoever/Who) takes us to the beach is my friend for life.

325. Do you know (what/where) happened to the rest of my tuna fish sandwich ?

326. At lunch, my friends and I talked about (what/which) we should do as our service project.

327. (That/Who) anyone could doubt their story seemed to amaze the children.

328. It's no use shutting the barn door (after/before) the horse is gone.

329. you gain strength, courage and confidence by every experience (in which/in what) you really stop to look fear in the face.

330. Let me not criticize any man (until/before) I have walked a mile in his moccasins.

331. They also serve (who/whom) only stand and wait.

332. Directors cannot always predict the reactions of the audience, (nor/or) can they always control the audience.

333. The workers in charge of properties are usually alert and efficient, (but/that) they do sometimes make mistakes.

334. Someday everyone might have the same enthusiasm for life on this planet, and then people (will take/would take) care of the environment.

335. The detective show appeared on television for several weeks (before/which) it became popular with viewers.

336. (After/While) we have written our report on the history of computers, we may be able to go to the picnic.

337. Neither of the plants (needs/need) water yet.

338. Two minutes (is/are) long enough to boil an egg.

339. My baseball and my catcher's mitt (are/is) back in my room.

340. All of the programs (have/has) been on television before.

341. One of the men (has/have) decided to get his car washed.

342. Have all the girls taken (their/her) projects home ?

343. Many of the trees had lost (their/its) leaves.

344. Every dog had a tag hanging from (its/their) collar.

345. A few of the carpenters had brought tools with (them/him).

346. According to the teacher, both of those titles should have lines drawn underneath (them/it).

347. My dog was among the winners in the show that had (their/its) picture taken.

348. No one was sure which of the streets had (their/its) names changed.

349. The launch of a space shuttle (attracts/attract) the interest of people throughout the world.

350. My favorite collection of poems (is/are) Where the Sidewalk Ends.

351. The starving children of the world (need/needs) food and medicine.

352. The thermos bottle in the picnic basket (is/are) filled with apple juice.

353. The chimes in the tower (play/plays) every hour.

354. The cucumbers in my garden (grow/grows) very quickly.

355. All of my friends (have/has) had the chicken pox.

356. Most of the appetizers on the restaurant menu (taste/tastes) delicious.

357. Everyone at the party (likes/like) the cottage cheese and vegetable dip.

358. Some of my classmates (take/takes) tennis lessons after school.

359. Nobody in the beginning painting class (displays/display) work in the annual art show.

360. All of the concert chorous members (harmonize/harmonizes) very well with each other.

361. Everybody (wants/want) to know who erected the massive stones.

362. All of the tourists (wonder/wonders) why the structure was built.

363. Last year a library and a museum (were/was) built in our town.

364. March and April (are/is) windy months.

365. Where (are/is) the bread and the honey ?

366. Our guava tree and our fig tree (bear/bears) more fruit than our entire neighborhood can eat.

367. Either the president or the vice-president of the class (calls/call) roll every morning.

368. Neither my sister nor I (mow/mows) the lawn without protesting.

369. The tulips and the daffodils (bloom/blooms) every April.

370. Either the squirrls or the dog (digs/dig) a new hole in the yard at least once a day.

371. None of the bricks (crack/cracks) if they are installed very carefully.

372. A car or camper (provides/provide) protection from animals.

373. Unfortunately, several of these generous people (have/has) been killed or maimed by the bears.

374. Most of the park's visitors now (realize/realizes) that wild bears are truly wild.

375. The family (were/was) arguing about where to spend the acting separately.

376. The crowd (are/is) straining to see the balloon.

377. (Here are/Here's) the answers to Chapter 8.

378. The public (differ/differs) in their opinions on the referendum.

379. (There are/There's) only three people in the contest.

380. (Where are/Where's) the bell peppers for the salad ?

381. My three-year-old sister (doesn't/don't) use good table manners.

382. They (don't/doesn't) have enough people to form a softball team.

383. (Doesn't/Don't) anyone know the time ?

384. Each of the ten-speed bicycles (costs/cost) over a hundred dollars.

385. Few of the boxers (leave/leaves) the ring without some bruises.

386. (Don't/Doesn't) you think three hours of homework is enough ?

387. Most of the puddle (disappears/disappear) after the sun comes out from behind the clouds.

388. Both of the doctors (agree/agrees) that she must have her tonsils removed.

389. Neither of those women got what (she/he) wanted.

390. Everyone in the class wanted to know (his/our) grade.

391. Nobody in the three classes would admit (his/their) guilt.

392. Neither the mother nor the daughter had forgotten (her/their) umbrella.

393. I am surprised that more people didn't volunteer to give (their/his) reports first.

394. Most of us wish that (we/she) did not have to give an oral report at all.

395. A few others in my class are going to try to get out of giving (their/his) reports at all.

396. The trees lost several of (their/its) branches in the thunderstorm last night.

397. The creek and the pond lost much of (their/its) water during the drought.

398. The fire engine and the police car went rushing by with (their/his) lights flashing.

399. Nearly every one of the girls in our class had (her/their) hair cut short.

400. Neither of those trees needs (its/their) limbs trimmed.

401. A person should weigh (his/their) words carefully before criticizing someone else.

402. Nearly every cat, no matter what breed, (goes/go) crazy for catnip.

403. Up until recently hardly anyone (has/have) been able to own a personal computer.

404. My spelling lessons and science homework sometimes (take/takes) me hours to finish.

405. The mice or the cat (has/have) eaten the cheese that was left out.

406. Why doesn't somebody raise (his/their) hand and ask for directions?

407. He does not go (to bed/bed) till past midnight.

408. One of the birds had lost most of (its/their) tail feathers.

409. Each of these tests has (its/their) own answer key.

410. Please ask some of these girls to pick up (their/her) own materials from the supply room.

411. In most cases, a dog or a cat that gets lost in the woods can take care of (itself/themselves).

412. I don't understand how chameleons sitting on a green leaf or a bush change (their/its) color.

413. The air conditioner and the refrigerator have switches that turn (them/it) off and on automatically.

414. No one could understand why Terry (chose/choose) the striped one instead of the others.

415. The waitress brought my order and (asked/asks) me if I wanted anything else.

416. The telephone (rang/rings) while I was in the shower.

417. The catfish (froze/freeze) in the pond last winter.

418. I (shrank/shrinked) down in the back seat so he wouldn't notice that I was laughing.

419. The waiter had brought our menus before we all (sat/sit) down.

420. We (drank/drunk) water with lemon slices in the glasses.

421. Carolyn (set/sat) her notebook on the kitchen counter.

422. The referee is (setting/sitting) the ball on the fifty-yard line.

423. My cat loves to (lie/lay) in the tall grass behind our house.

424. The newspaper had (lain/lay) in the yard until the sun faded it.

425. The steam was (rising/raising) from the pot of hot chicken soup on the stove.

426. My father promised to (raise/rise) my allowance if I pull the weeds.

427. The student body's interest in this subject has (risen/raised) to new heights.

428. Key West (lies/lays) off the southwestern coast of Florida.

429. When the sun had (set/sit), I wearily (lay/laid) on the hard earth in my tent.

430. Your grades must (rise/raise), or you will not make the honor roll this term.

431. He left his books (lying/laying) on the table.

432. We had (ridden/rode) halfway across the desert when I began to wish I had (brought/brung) more water.

433. If that had happened to me, I would have (frozen/freeze) with fear.

434. Several mechanics worked on my aunt's car before one of them finally (found/finds) the problem.

435. The wasp flew in the window and bit (him/he) on the arm.

436. We thought that we'd be facing (them/they) in the finals.

437. The best soloists in the band are (they/them), apparently.

438. Everyone belived it was (we/us) students.

439. It might have been (he/him), but I'm not sure.

440. If the singer had been (she/her), I would have listened.

441. The mayor congratulated (us/we) volunteers for our effort.

442. The film editor showed the visitors and (us/we) students around the television station.

443. Tomorrow you and (they/them) can distribute posters.

444. Where should you (I/me) meet after school ?

445. Please invite your cousin and (them/they) to the horse show this Saturday.

446. Members of the decorating committee for the dance include four juniors and (us/we).

447. I wrote a story about my great-grandmother and (him/he).

448. When my mother finally found me sitting on the curb, she was mad at (me/I).

449. The shop teacher said he was pleased with (me/I).

450. At the movies we met Julia and (her/she) while buying popcorn.

451. My mother never tires of telling Mary Anne and (me/I) what it was like

when she was our age.

452. I (couldn't/couldn't hardly) believe she said that.

453. They offer so many combinations that I don't know which one I like (most/more).

454. There's nothing I like (more/more better) than barbecued ribs.

455. Why doesn't the teacher give us questions that are (easier/more easier).

456. New York City has a larger population than (any other city/any city) in the United States.

457. Gina has more ideas for the festival than (anyone else/anyone).

458. My uncle served in the U.S. Army during the (War/war) in Vietnam.

459. The American (Revolution/revolution) took place toward the end of the Age of Englightenment in the eighteenth century.

460. The (South American/south american) rain forests contain many different kinds of plants and animals.

461. The language most widely spoken in (Brazil/brazil) is (Portuguese /portuguese).

462. Does anyone know where the crank that we use to open the top window (is?/is.)

463. After the rain stopped (falling,/falling) the blue jays hopped around the lawn in search of worms.

464. My cousin will stay here (tonight,/tonight) or they will drive on to Aunt Cindy's house.

465. (Jupiter,/Jupiter) the fifth planet from the (sun,/sun) is so large that all the other planets in our solar system would fit inside it.

466. The coach (advises/advices) us to stick to the training rules.

467. Do you think my work is (all right/alright) ?

468. The Amazon River is longer (than/then) the Mississippi River.

469. If the baby is awake by four o'clock, we will leave (then/than).

470. My jacket is made of a new (synthetic/imitation) material.

471. The monks in several medieval monasteries kept (annals/histories) summarizing the important events of each year.

472. You can imagine how (humiliating/ shaming) it was to be spanked in front of all my relatives.

473. Although the lawer stayed within the law, he relied on (guile/fraud) to win his case.

474. After studying the problem I formed a working (hypothesis/theory), which I tested by experiment.

475. The young couple fondly (fed/sustained) their baby daughter.

476. Our (invincible/victorious) army never has been and never should be defeated in battle.

477. Lobsters, the delight of many diners, are large shellfish that live (in/that) the sea.

478. They use small, specially constructed bots and a number (of/which) cratelike traps made (of/what) wood.

479. Farmers used the plentiful lobsters as fertilizer (for/where) their gardens.

480. The location (of/as) the traps is marked (with/who) colorful floats; the colors, which are registered, identify the owners.

481. A lobster (with/about) only one claw is called a "cull"; one (without/to) any claws is called a "pistol" or "buffalo."

482. On the second load, either Fred (or/nor) my father slipped, and the refrigerator fell on Father's foot.

483. Father's enthusiasm was somewhat dimmed, (yet/so) he said his foot didn't hurt much and we were still doing a wonderful job.

484. A number of people (have/has) tried to photograph the monster, without success.

485. This fearsome monster reportedly (chases/chase) campers and wayward travelers through the woods.

486. This legendary humanlike creature (secludes/seclude) itself in heavily

forested areas.

487. There are many (questions/question) on American history in my book.

488. There (are/is) many often-told jokes and riddles.

489. There (are/is) a dozen eggs and a pound of butter left.

490. The marching band practiced hard and (won/wins) the state competition.

491. The newborn calf rose to its feet with a wobbling motion and (stood/stands) for the first time.

492. The (prancing/prancie) horses were loudly applauded by the delighted audience.

493. (Swaggering/Swagger) and boasting, he made the entire team extremely angry.

494. (Leaving/Leave) the field, the happy player rushed to her parents sitting in the bleachers.

495. We thought the (banging/bange) shutter upstairs was someone walking in the attic.

496. (Terrified/Terrify) by our big dog, the burglar turned and fled.

497. (Walking/Walk) is an exercise for everyone, young or old.

498. At today's practice we concentrated on (passing/pass) the ball.

499. The sophomores are enjoying (woodworking/woodwork) this semester.

500. His job is (giving/gives) the customers their memus.

501. (To dance/Dancing) gracefully requires coordination.

502. A good way (to lose/losing) weight is (to eat/eating) moderately.

503. The best way (to get/getting) there is (to take/taking) the bus.

504. If you were (to review/reviewing) a recent movie, which would you select ?

505. (Sold/Selling) to P.T. Barnum in 1882, Jumbo was sent to the United States.

506. Unfortunnately, only seven of Emily's poems were (published/publishing) while she was alive.

507. This is the new music (video that/video, that) I like best.

508. (Griffins, which/Griffins which) are mythological beasts, are seen on many

coats of arms.

509. The students questioned the (data on/data, on) which the theory was based.

510. The public (wants/want) more information about the candidates in this election.

511. I can't read Steven's poem because there (are/is) too many smudges on the paper.

512. Few of the people here for vacation (want/wants) to live here year-round.

513. The confusion among shoppers (is/are) certainly understandable.

514. For example, the quantity printed on yogurt containers (tells/tell) the number of onces in a container.

515. Different brands of juice (show/shows) the same quantity in different ways.

516. Shoppers' confusion, along with rising prices, (is/are) a matter of concern to consumer groups.

517. The units in this system (have/has) a relationship to one another.

518. Consumer groups in this country (continue/continues) to advocate a uniform system of measurement.

519. The metric system, in use in European countries, (solves/solve) most of the confusion.

520. One can with a label showing twenty-four ounces (contains/contain) the same quantity as a can with a label showing one pint eight ounces.

521. A shopper on the lookout for bargains (does not/do not) know whether liquid or solid measure is indicated.

522. The traditional system of indicating quantities (makes/make) shopping a guessing game.

523. The catcher should have (thrown/throw) the ball to first base.

524. The wind (blew/blows) all night.

525. No one except Bill and (her/she) went to the fair.

526. Everyone at the dance contest applauded the winning couple, Marco and (her/she).

527. Can you give Teresa and (me/I) directions to State Street ?

528. One of the guides asked Sean and (me/I) if (we/Us) boys wanted to operate the computer.

529. (She/Her) and her twin sister were demonstrating the machines.

530. Judith and (she/her) gave (us/we) boys a chance to dance with the robot, too.

531. Just between you and (me/I) this desert is too sweet.

532. Everyone except you and (her/she) is wearing a costume.

533. (He/Him) and (I/me) are working on a special project.

534. When are your parents and (they/them) coming home ?

535. The teacher gave James and (me/I) extra math homework.

536. The woman (to whom/to who) I was speaking is conducting a survey.

537. Anyone (who/whom) misses the bus will be penalized by the coach.

538. Her grandmother, to (whom/who) she sent the flowers, won the over-fifty marathon.

539. Both of women (who/whom) ran for election to the city council were elected.

540. That author (whom/who) you admire is scheduled to visit the local bookstore next Tuesday.

541. Sometimes it was difficult to tell who was having a better time, (they/them) or (we/us).

542. It is unlikely that Betty and (I/me) can make enough money this summer to pay for a trip to the Canadian Rockies.

543. (He/Him) and his father are taking a class in microwave cooking at a local appliance store.

544. Writing a mystery story is the (most/more) challenging assignment I've had so far.

545. Everyone seemed greatly (affected/effected) by her gracious thank-you note.

546. I've spent all my money.　(Besides/Beside), I've already seen that movie.

547. My schedule this year includes English, social studies, science, (etc./and etc.)

548. Did you (take/bring) flowers to your aunt when you visited her in her new home ?

549. Is that (as fast as/all the faster) you can read ?

550. (Everywhere/Everywheres) we went there were long lines.

551. My motion to adjourn the meeting was not (accepted/excepted) by the president.

552. Perhaps I should (have/of) called before coming to see you at your home.

553. Perhaps the young couple (ought not/hadn't ought) to have married at all.

554. The death of Romeo and Juliet (taught/learned) the Montagues and the Capulets a bitter lesson and finally ended the feud.

555. (Unless/Without) it stops snowing, we'll have to call off the hike.

556. Someone hand me (those/them) nails and (that/that there) hammer.

557. I read (that/where) Roanoke Island isn't (anywhere/anywheres) near Roanoke, Virginia.

558. (Those/Them) jars of homemade preserves should be stored in a cool place.

559. Is she the player (who/which) is favored to win at Wimbledon this year ?

560. He would not have released the report (unless/without) he had first verified his sources.

561. I (have/haven't) borrowed but one book from the library this week.

562. By the time we wrote for tickets, there weren't (any/none) left.

563. Didn't you (ever/never) told (anyone/no one) about our discovery.

564. The park is two blocks west of the (Methodist/methodist) church.

565. Frank and Ellen will take (Chemistry/chemistry) II next year, but I will take (Latin/latin) instead.

566. After (Hurricane/hurricane) (Allen/allen) struck, the governor declared the region a disaster area.

567. The summer games of the 1984 (Olympics/olympics) were held in (Los Angeles/los angeles), California.

568. Use light colors (, by the way,/by the way) to make a small room seem larger.

569. The sun danced over the(cool, dark/cool dark) water and shone through the branches of the tall pine trees.

570. Joe asked me who was bringing the plastic forks, (paper plates,/paper plates) and Styrofoam cups to the picnic.

571. (Well,/Well) that's the last time I ever ride in a car with my brother (Ted!/Ted)

572. The (batter, hoping/batter hoping) to advance the runners (,laid/laid) down a perfect bunt.

573. Humans (, one kind of living organism,/one kind of living organism) affect their environment in both beneficial and harmful ways.

574. The mayor (, a member of the audience, /a member of the audience) soon promised to appoint a committee to correct the problem.

575. (Consequently,/Consequently) people will exercise by walking or by riding bicycles.

576. Did you know that this lovely flower is a (bluebonnet,/bluebonnet) a variety of wild (lupine?/lupine.)

577. (Theirs/Theirs') is the only house with blue shutters, so you should have no difficulty finding it.

578. Penny and Arline worked as gardeners this summer and saved (their/they're) money for a ski trip.

579. The students (whose/who's) names are called are to report backstage.

580. (One's/Ones) teeth should be checked regularly.

581. He added (one-half/one half) teaspoon of vanilla to the mixture and set the timer for (thirty-five/thirty five) minutes.

582. After the long war, (peace/piece) was welcome.

583. Everyone was (formally/formerly) dressed at the dance.

584. Tell me (whether/weather) or not we won.

585. You should not consider this a (waste/waist) of time.

586. If you decide (to go, I'll go with you./to go.)

587. (She was elected/Elected) by an overwhelming number of the students.

588. Because they wanted to escape the (heat, they/heat.   They) left for the (mountains, setting/mountains.   Setting) out in the early part of August.

589. The large but sluggish panda is not (known/knows) as a successful hunter of small animals.

590. The radio (sends/send) the scientists valuable information about the released animal's behavior.

591. A speech community is a group of people (who/at) speak the same language.

592. There are speech communities (that/in) consist of millions of people and some that contain only a few hundred.

593. People (who/which) conduct business internationally should know more than one language.

594. In one corner we stacked a mound of debris (so that/so) it could be hauled away.

595. Long hours in the hot sun had made us feel (as though/as) the day would never end.

596. The jury (has/have) been paying close attention to the evidence in this case.

597. There (are/is) four herbs that any gardener can grow; basil, thyme, marjoram, and oregano.

598. All of these old letters (were/was) tied with ribbon and stored in a trunk in the attic.

599. Neither potatoes nor corn (is/are) grown on this farm.

600. Two students from each class (is/are) going to the state capital to attend a special conference on education.

601. Although she owns several pieces of fine china, her most prized possession (are/is) the little cups inherited from a great-aunt.

602. The members of the family (meet/meets) for a reunion every year.

603. The escape of three snakes from the laboratory (has/have) created quite a stir.

604. The chief, along with two of the firefighters, (gives/give) lectures on home safety.

605. Participation in class discussions, not just high test scores, (counts/count) toward one's final grade.

606. Our class or theirs (is/are) going to sponsor the dance.

607. Every one of these handy mango peelers (comes/come) with a one-year guarantee.

608. Two thirds of a cup of flour (is/are) needed for this recipe.

609. There (are/is), in my opinion, a number of good reasons for the proposed change.

610. After the long hike through the woods, all of the scouts complained that (their/his) feet hurt.

611. Some of the women wrote to (their/her) local newspapers about the pollution problem.

612. Many of the crew got (their/his) first case of seasickness in the violent storm.

613. One of the houses had (its/their) windows broken by the hail.

614. An additional feature of these models (is/are) the built-in stereo speakers.

615. One of the goats (was/were) nibbling on a discared popcorn box.

616. If anyone comes in now, (he/they) will see what a mess we've made.

617. Where (is/are) the box of nails that came with the kit ?

618. A few of our classmates (were/was) invited.

619. There (is/are) leftover macaroni and cheese on the top shelf in the refrigerator.

620. If anybody likes a spectacle, (he/they) will love seeing a drum corps competition.

621. A philosopher once said that if someone built a better mousetrap, the world would beat a path to (his/their) door.

622. A hostile crowd gathered outside the courtroom to show (its/their) disapproval of the verdict.

623. All of the bread (is/are) on the table.

624. I need to know today if you and (she/her) plan to go with us on the trip.

625. I am going to vote for (whoever/whomever) can present the best solution to environmental problems.

626. After the bake sale, give the remaining cookies and cakes to everyone (who/whom) worked.

627. Before the debate started, I noticed that my opponent was as nervous as (I/me).

628. Seeing a car with an out-of-state license plate in my driveway, I ran inside, and (who/whom) do you think was there ?

629. We watched another canoeist and saw how (she/her) and her partner maneuvered their craft.

630. Susan grabbed for our sleeping bags, and (she/her) and (I/me) both scrambled for our food cooler.

631. My father warning haunted all of (us/we) as (we/us) starved adventurers stared at waterlogged hot dogs, soaked rolls, and biscuits with tadpoles in them.

632. The wary skunk circled around (her/she) and (me/I).

633. She praised her compatriots, from (whom/who) new advances in agriculture had recently come.

634. The coach asked you and (me/I) for help with the team's new equipment.

635. The electrician warned (him/he) and (me/I) about the frayed wires.

636. The author, (whom/who) the critics had praised, autographed a copy of his

novel for me.

637. The sleet whirled about George and (him/he) until they could barely see.

638. The dirty dishes had (lain/laid) in the sink for hours.

639. Were you (lying/laying) down for a while before dinner ?

640. The dough for the biscuits was (rising/raising) in the bowl on the sill.

641. People who live along this road complain because it is the (worst/worstest) in the entire township.

642. She felt (bad/badly) because she had not recovered from the illness and could not play with the team.

643. Finding that the new map was (more, useful/usefuller) to me than my old one, I took it with me in the car.

644. The red apples in that basket are (sweeter/more sweeter) than the green ones you bought yesterday.

645. (Since/Being that) everyone is here, let's begin.

646. The crosslike rays radiating from the moon were an (illusion/allusion) caused by the screen door.

647. The heat has affected the growing season; we'll harvest (fewer/less) crops this year.

648. You could (have/of) borrowed the books from me.

649. We didn't want to take the boat out because the waves looked (rather/sort of) choppy.

650. A solar eclipse (occurs/is) when the moon comes between the earth and the sun.

651. A run-on sentence (means that/is where) two sentences are erroneously joined as one.

652. They were the very ones (who/which) complained about the achievement test.

653. Betty heard on the radio (that/where) the mayor is going to Washington about the redevelopment project.

654. Linda (doesn't/don't) enjoy doing (that/them) sort of exercise.

655. My grandmother (emigrated/immigrated) from Italy as a young woman.

656. We made (this/this here) maple syrup on our own farm.

657. Would you like to be the first student to ride in a (space shuttle/Space Shuttle) that orbits the earth ?

658. (Gloria,/Gloria) did you see where I left my bowling ball ?

659. My cousin, a mail (carrier, does/carrier does) not like jokes about postal workers.

660. At the gymnastics meet Lees performed on the parallel bars, (the rings, and/the rings and) the high bar.

661. They phrased the petition carefully and presented it at the requested (time; however/time however), the governor ignored it.

662. We took some food to the stray (dog; it/dog it) looked so forlorn standing in the doorway.

663. None of the entries that were submitted met the standard of quality the art museum expected for the (contest; therefore/contest therefore), no winner was named.

664. The directions were as (follows; remove/follows remove) plastic wrap, place in oven, and bake for thirty minutes.

665. Do you know (who's/whose) responsible for (their/they're) leaving ?

666. I know (you're/your) upset with the plan, but (it's/its) the only way to solve the problem.

667. Around his (waist/waste) he wore a handmade leather belt.

668. (Whether/Weather) or not it rains or snows, we will be there.

669. Over the centuries, English (has borrowed/have borrowed) many words from other languages.

670. Because a newly borrowed word (sounds/sound) unfamiliar, people sometimes do not hear it correctly.

671. Actual facts concerning his life (remain/remains) few.

672. Boswell's book, unlike many of the full-length biographies of the next century, (was/were) an accurate and faithful record.

673. His sensitive ear (could detect/to detect) even the smallest change.

674. Two of the books (had been/had) torn.

675. I (haven't seen/haven't) a winter like that in seventeen years.

676. (Having/Have) been aided by warm weather and clear skies, the sailors rejoiced as they arrived on time.

677. I would love to see (it bursting/ it bursts) into bloom in the spring; it must be quite a sight !

678. We discovered an antique shop with unusual objects (to sell/selling).

679. Please list the names of all the (people/person) to whom we should go for help.

680. Basketball, like many other games, (offers/offer) enjoyment and exercise to all who participate.

681. Scurvy, one of the diseases modern science has conquered, (results/result) from a lack of vitamin C.

682. Many who give their time to help the disabled (work/works) as volunteers at the Special Olympics.

683. Neither of my sisters owns (her/their) own pair of ice skates.

684. The beauty of trees in their fall colors (attracts/attract) many tourists to New England.

685. Other animals besides the elephant (are/is) classified as pachyderms.

686. Some of the software for our computer (is/are) arriving late.

687. Others besides you and me (advocate/advocates) a town cleanup day.

688. The effective date of the new regulations for nuclear power plants (has/have) not yet been determined.

689. The idea that they do not wear out or have to be flipped over (makes/make) compact discs attractive.

690. The debate over the rule changes (has/have) apparently thrown the meeting

into a deadlock.

691. The public education system for boys and girls in the United States (is/are) intended to stress basic skills.

692. Perhaps the best thing about calculators (is/are) their speed in arriving at accurate answers.

693. One sixth of the budget (is/are) allocated to health care.

694. (Does/Do) every boy and girl in the city schools vote in the student council elections ?

695. Measles (is/are) less prevalent now that children can be inoculated against the disease.

696. Students who are not finished taking the exam (don't/doesn't) appreciate loud noises in the corridors.

697. The unusual phenomena (were/was) explained by astronomers as being caused by sunsports.

698. It is difficult to make a choice because there (are/is) so many styles of tennis shoes.

699. The list of the best ballplayers of all time (is/are) dominated by-outfielders.

700. The Mexican peso, worth approximately one-half cent (is/are) easily accepted by the present toll machines.

701. A school handbook is given to all who (enroll/enrolls) in our school.

702. Nobody left the prom early, because they were enjoying (themselves/himself).

703. Half the members of my history class this year (are/is) in the National Honor Society.

704. Advances in medical research (have/has) nearly eradicated many childhood diseases.

705. The answer that people who like them (give/gives) is that they never wear out because needles never touch them.

706. To learn more about our city government, our civics class (plans/plan) to

invite various guest speakers to school.

707. Included on our list (are/is) the mayor, a lawer, a probation officer, a police officer, and a local or state representive.

708. Listening to guest speakers explain and discuss their jobs (makes/make) the class period pass quickly.

709. Please write and tell my mother and (me/I) about your vacation.

710. I thought that the best tennis players in my school were my cousin Adele and (he/him).

711. My great-grandmother, my grandfather, and (I/myself) have had some good talks together.

712. (She and I/Her and me) lent him our American history books.

713. (Whom/Who) did you talk to at the information desk ?

714. These photographs were taken by John and (her/she).

715. The captain tried to steer the ship between the lighthouse and (them/they).

716. She gave the sports assignment for the school newspaper to Frank and (me/I).

717. The author of the story never tells us whether it was (she/her) or her sister who won the contest.

718. When will you learn that (we/us) drivers must stay within the speed limit ?

719. Pearl Buck is a novelist (whom/who) most Americans are familiar with.

720. Science had always given Joan and (me/I) trouble.

721. (We/Us) two job seekers found a number of ads for computer operators.

722. Was it (she/her) (whom/who) the guidance counselor called to her office.

723. The title of salutatorian goes to (whoever/whomever) has the second highest academic average.

724. Our instructor was a successful mechanic (whom/who) all of us came to appreciate.

725. Do you have time to show Larry and (us/we) how to change the oil ?

726. Edward said that he too wanted (to go/to have gone) to the beach yesterday.

727. If I (were/was) you, I would not skate on that lake; the ice is too thin.

728. Since last September I (have missed/missed) only one day of school.

729. The house became very quiet after everyone (had left/left)

730. The crowded roots of the plant (burst/bursted) the flowerpot.

731. The cassette tape deck (must have broken/must have broke) this morning.

732. They have (rung/ringed) the bell in front of the school twelve consecutive times.

733. In New York City, buildings that are officially designated landmarks cannot be (torn/teared) down.

734. Was the tape deck (stolen/stole) out of her car ?

735. The potted plant was (blown/blow) over by a gust of wind.

736. Each of us had (chosen/chose) a different American writer.

737. (Lie/Lay) here and relax before going on.

738. Earthquakes may occur wherever the fault (lies/lays).

739. She read the paper as she (lay/laid) in the recliner.

740. We all (sat/set) around the campfire last night.

741. Should we (sit/set) here in the sun, or do you prefer the shade ?

742. The woman who is (rising/raising) in the audience has been nominated for vice-president.

743. Those watermelons had (lain/laid) in the field a week, ready to be put onto the trucks.

744. The package is (lying/laying) inside the storm door.

745. He has (laid/lain) his racquetball glove on the bench.

746. This summer our squash vines have grown so profusely that they (have taken/have took) over almost the entire garden.

747. My favorite scene in the movie was the one in which the comic hero (bit/bited) the dog.

748. By the time we get to the picnic area, the rain (will have stopped/Will Stop).

749. In August my parents (will have been married/will be married) for twenty-five years.

750. I would have agreed if you (had asked/would have asked) me sooner.

751. If the books (were cataloged/have been cataloged) last week, why haven't they been placed on the shelves ?

752. Who has not heard that there (are/were) a thousand meters in a kilometer ?

753. The book is on works of art that (were created/have been created) centuries ago.

754. If I (had listened/would have listened) more carefully, I might have taken better notes.

755. The lobbyists (had been waiting/were waiting) an hour before the governor arrived.

756. If he (had revised/would have revised) his first draft, he would have received a better grade.

757. When you charge the battery in the car, be sure (to protect/to have protected) your eyes and hands from the sulfuric acid in the battery.

758. Before next Saturday is over, we (will have heard/will hear) some exciting music at the concert.

759. My old skates (have lain/lay) in my closet for the past two years.

760. If you (had remembered/would have remembered) to bring something to read, you would not have been bored.

761. The smell from the paper mill (lay/laid) over the town like a blanket.

762. After the scout had seen the wide receiver in action, he wished he (had offered/offered) the player a scholarship.

763. By the time we (smelled/had smelled) the smoke, the flames had already begun to spread.

764. I (am/be) glad to have the opportunity to revise my essay for a higher grade.

765. Even though her standards (were/would be) high, she was considered the

most popular teacher in the school.

766. If I (had seen/would have seen) the accident, I would have reported it to the police.

767. From our studies we (concluded/had concluded) that women had played many critical roles in the history of our nation.

768. By the time you leave high school, you (will have learned/will learn) many interesting facts about history.

769. How many of us possess the skills (to survive/to have survived) on our own without the assistance of store-bought items ?

770. If you (had taken/would have taken) a nutrition class, you would have learned how to shop wisely for food.

771. Judy, my pet chipmunk, was acting as if she (were/was) trying to tell me something.

772. After spending the entire morning working in the garden, Jim (is lying/is laying) down for a rest.

773. This has been the most (wonderful/wonderfullest) day of my life.

774. This car is roomier than (any other/any) car we ever had.

775. As you approach the intersection, drive (cautiously/cautious).

776. You will drive more (steadily/steady) if you keep your eyes on the road.

777. Both books are rare, but the one bound in green cloth is the (less/least) valuable one.

778. My geometry grades were higher than (anyone else's/anyone's) in my class.

779. This engine is twelve years old, but it still runs (well/good).

780. Yesterday our classroom computer was acting rather (strangely/strange).

781. Some machines break down (continually/continual), while others almost never need repairs.

782. If you enunciate (clearly/clear), people will be able to understand what you are saying.

783. I tried to explain why I was late, but my mother looked at me

(skeptically/skeptical).

784. When my parents correct my little sister, they tell her not to behave (badly/bad).

785. Don't feel (bad/badly) if any of these sentences have tricked you; you are not alone !

786. The members of our school's volleyball team get along (well/good) together.

787. After school, go home (quickly/quick) to catch the TV special.

788. When we have Italian food for supper, Joe eats more (than anyone else/than anyone) at the table.

789. I know this shade of blue is a closer much than that one, but we still haven't found the (best match/better match).

790. Which of the four shorthand dictations was the (hardest/harder) ?

791. I'm glad you are taking grammar study more (seriously/serious).

792. Megan shoots foul so (well/good) that she has made first-string varsity.

793. When I got economics test back, I found I had done (worse/more badly) than I had feared.

794. This fast-food restaurant advertises that its hamburgers are (bigger/more bigger) than anyone else's.

795. After receiving a rare coin for my birthday, I began to take coin collecting (more seriously/serious).

796. When Mrs. Hayes calls on me in chemistry class, I can't help (feeling/but feel) nervous and uncertain.

797. I (could/couldn't) hardly believe my eyes when I saw a 90 on my geometry test; I must (have/of) remembered the formulas better than I thought I would.

798. It looks (as if/like) it will pour any minute.

799. (Can't any/Can't none) of the people in town see that the mayor is appointing political cronies to patronage jobs.

800. What (kind of/kind of a) person would assassinate the President of the United States ?

801. A large (number/amount) of scarlet fever cases have been reported.

802. She found spelling errors (everywhere/everywheres) as she began to profread her late ?

803. Please (take/bring) your belongings with you when you go.

804. This is (as far as/all the farther) this old car can take us.

805. How can we three divide a dollar equally (among/between) ourselves.

806. I didn't guess until the last chapter that the butler (did/done) it.

807. Try to make your drawing (like/as) the one on the chart.

808. I read in a newspaper article (that/where) dogs are being trained to help deaf people.

809. The swings in the park are rusting (somewhat/some).

810. Since I didn't have (any/no) homework, I decided to go out to shoot some baskets.

811. Tom didn't do (anything/nothing) to help us with the dinner.

812. The lights were so dim that we (could barely/couldn't barely) see anything.

813. In the mountains you (can't help feeling/can't help but feel) calm.

814. (Besides/Beside) my job as a baby sitter, I work as a hospital volunteer.

815. If you kept (fewer/less) fish in your tank, they would live longer.

816. Leave the theater (immediately!/immediately?)

817. The leopard can't change (its/it's) spots.

818. Mary is the girl (whose/who's) mother I met.

819. Did you try on those (clothes/cloths) before you paid for them ?

820. When her painting was purchased by the museum, the artist received many (compliments/complements).

821. One of my father's favorite sayings is "What's next--- (dessert/desert) or (desert/dessert) the table ?"

822. I enjoy both chicken and steak but prefer the (latter/later).

823. Literature and composition are the (principal/principle) parts of the course.

824. The accident that completely demolished the car was caused by a (loose/lose) cotter pin worth ten cents.

825. If that is not (your/you're) car, (whose/who's) is it ---- (theirs/there's) ?

826. Although you present a convincing (argument, I/argument I) will not change my mind.

827. When Elsie received the reply in the (mail, she/mail she) tore open the envelope impatiently.

828. We must see the objects (themselves/himself) as shapes instead of thinking about their funtion.

829. Most of us block out (our/ourselves) everyday surroundings.

830. Our old car needs either a valve job (or/nor) a new engine.

831. Both Mike (and/or) Sue work at the same supermarket.

832. She is (someone who/someone, who) has shown remarkable courage.

833. This book, which I read for my history (report, is/report is) about Africa.

834. The amplifier was (one that/one, that) we had seen before.

835. Let's listen to a weather (forecaster whom/forecaster who) we can trust.

836. I know how you are feeling, (and I/I) am happy for you.

837. The problem is that my finances don't quite allow me to live in style; (in fact,/and) I'm broke.

838. Ask someone who knows toys (what/that) their enchantment is worth.

839. (Although this/This) dish is usually served with rice, Lola and her father prepared a green salad instead.

840. What, they asked, (would/will) the computer do ?

841. (There/They) are certain elements in literary research that computer can pick up faster than readers can.

842. A team with too many superstars (has/have) trouble working as a unit.

843. "(Is/Are) mumps contagious ? " I asked when my sister got the disease two days before I was star in our school play.

844. Many a financial investor (has/have) a headache on a day when the stock market drops.

845. The number of people seeking jobs in the computer industry (is/are) rising rapidly.

846. My mother thought twenty-five dollars (was/were) too much to pay for the designer T-shirt.

847. One of the women hurt (her/their) foot in the race.

848. The theory of plate tectonics (has/have) explained causes of earthquake activity throughout the world.

849. The pressure of colliding plates (forces/force) the rock to bend until it breaks.

850. The scientific community, especially seismologists and geologists, (is/are) studing the effects of earthquakes.

851. All of our belongings (are/is) still unpacked.

852. A band with two trumpet players and thirty-five clarinetists (sounds/sound) terrible.

853. The cause of the recent fires (is/are) being investigated.

854. None of the students (have disagreed/has disagreed) with my suggestion.

855. The water supply for all the states (comes/come) from either surface water or underground water.

856. Not one of the water sources (is/are) free from pollution.

857. In some regions, the drinking water for hundreds of people (comes/come) from aquifers.

858. Ground water in some areas (is/are) being used faster than the supply can be renewed.

859. Each one of the fifty states (has/have) a stake in preserving sources of water.

860. The United States (was/were) represented at the summit conference.

861. Many a young runner (finishes/finish) the grueling race in less than five

hours.

862. The captain of the football team and the president of the senior class (represent/represents) the students.

863. Every volunteer in the city's hospitals (is/are) being honored at the banquet.

864. That was one of those jokes that (offend/offends) everyone.

865. The number of serious accidents that (happen/happens) at home is surprisingly large.

866. The company advertises (its/their) products on television.

867. As far as I could see, neither of the women made a mistake while presenting (her/their) argument during the debate.

868. This is one of those cars that (have/has) a fuel injection system.

869. Three fourths of the audience always (stays/stay) until the last note is played.

870. All but three games in the final round (were/was) held at the community center.

871. When one of the teachers (retires/retire), the students give him an engraved plaque.

872. The factory of the future (will have/have) robots working on its assembly line.

873. (Are/Is) there any milk and apple pie in the refrigerator ?

874. Every file cabinet, bookcase, and desk drawer (was/were) crammed with books and papers.

875. Some of the information found in reference books (needs/need) to be updated every year.

876. None of the competitors knew what (their/his) own chances of winning were.

877. My parents have a low tolerance for (my/me) playing rock music.

878. The bus driver always greeted (us/we) students with smile.

879. The President-elect knew exactly (whom/who) he wanted to appoint as Secretary of State.

880. The teacher gave her friend and (her/she) more homework.

881. The slide show was presented by my sister and (me/I).

882. Is it really (she/her) walking down the road ?

883. During the busy season, the boss relies on (us/we) workers.

884. Who is running toward (him/he) ?

885. We did not hear (whom/who) the principal had named.

886. Anybody (who/whom) orders now will receive a free gift.

887. Several of the women (who/whom) had served on committees were considered.

888. Anyone (whom/who) she can corner will be treated to a lecture on buying a home computer.

889. The player's reaction was to shout at the referee (who/whom) charged him with the penalty.

890. Did you object to (my making/me make) through the woods ?

891. My close friends, Judy and (she/her), joined the choir.

892. Also, we thought wrongly that (her/she) sitting in for him would decrease our work load.

893. Well, I'm sure you can guess (whom/who) the situation taught a lesson to.

894. It's funny how even an assistant supervisor can make her meaning clear to people like (us/ourselves) in just a few sentences.

895. If I (had/would have) told the truth in the first place, the situation would have been much easier to handle.

896. The five riders are pleased (to have qualified/to qualify) for the equestrian team.

897. I wished that there (were/was) a good movie playing in town.

898. Some of the sketches (were drawn/were drew) with pen and ink.

899. The farmer (has driven/has drived) that old tractor nearly every day for

twenty years.

900. The children's choir (sang/sung) as well as could be expected.

901. If they (had called/would have called) sooner, I would have given them a ride.

902. If she (had forgotten/forgot) the directions, we could have been lost.

903. As I thought about our argument, I was sure you (had lost/lost) your temper first.

904. We wanted (to avoid/to have avoided) any controversy.

905. By the time dinner was ready, I (had done/did) all my math homework.

906. As soon as we returned to the campsite, we discovered that someone (had taken/took) our food and gear.

907. If we (had had/would have had) the engine tuned, I'm sure we would not be stranded on the highway now.

908. If we (had checked/would have checked), we'd have known the store was closed.

909. I never realized that hurricanes and typhoons (are/were) really the same thing.

910. If we (had had/had) the chance, we would have stopped by your house.

911. When you get to the stop sign, turn (sharply/sharp) to the left.

912. The room won't look so (bad/badly) after it has been painted.

913. The lizard turned its head so (slowly/slow) that it looked as if it weren't moving at all.

914. The understudy seemed (nervous/nervously) to the audience.

915. People need to develop a (clearer/more clear) sense of self-worth.

916. Dividing the pie in two, Wilson took (the lesser/the least) and gave me the larger portion.

917. After a hot day, a cold glass of water tastes (good/well).

918. I have narrowed my choices to two colleges, and I want to visit them to see which I like (better/best).

919. He inched very (gradually/gradual) toward the doorway.

920. It is often said that beauty (is only/only) skin deep.

921. Because it was (likely/liable) to rain, John canceled his plans to go swimming.

922. The reason we are moving is (that/because) my parents have always wanted to live in Taipei.

923. Whenever I'm not doing (something/nothing) challenging, I grow bored easily.

924. I'm probably getting the flu, because I have felt (nauseated/nauseous) all day long.

925. The reason we're so late is (that/because) our car wouldn't start.

926. (Naturally,/Naturally) the seafood that I like best, lobster, is also the most expensive.

927. A large crowd walked (up/where) the stairs in the history building.

928. Surprised by the house owner's return, the intruder hurried (through/what) the door.

929. The unfortunate children were scattered (among/what) many homes.

930. Successful training taps (into/that) an employee's knowledge and experience.

931. The grateful veteran relaxed in his living room (after/when) years of battle.

932. I think I (have figured/figured) out a solution to this problem.

933. Travel (has become/became) so expensive over the past few years that we can no longer afford it.

934. The man (whom/who) you called is out and his assistant insists that he will not return again today.

935. (Who/Whom) does what to whom in each day's story is very important.

936. Please call Henry and (me/I) as soon as you know the election returns.

937. I must insist that I do like (your/you) smoking in my home.

938. If anyone can be consistently supportive of students, it is (she/her).

939. For as long as I have known her, (she/her) has been a model teacher.

940. Many people believe in stronger consumer protection and better (consumer/our) products.

941. (Unless/Until) you give me all the data by September 23, the report won't be in on time.

942. Both procedures are costly, not only in dollars, (but also/and) in energy use.

943. Many children are fed more than necessary, (and they/they) have many unnecessary sweets on their menus.

944. We decided to play tennis, have lunch, (and play/play) bridge.

945. The babysitter gave the child lunch, and (the child/she) continued to play.

946. I had difficulty with the spinning (wheel because/what) I had never tried one before.

947. The graduates and their teachers gathered in the auditorium, (where/which) the graduates received their diplomas.

948. I bought the outfit because (it was/was) on sale.

949. The polite time to comment (came after/comes after) he had finished his speech.

950. Since I (had cooked/cooked) dinner, we did not go out to eat.

951. Mom, I don't know (why, it/why it) was there when I tried to clean it with the vacuum cleaner.

952. The (ex-Senator/ex senator) hoped that approval of his protege's bill would pass the two-thirds mark.

953. Our (history/History) course this semester highlights civilizations of the (East/east).

954. Each year our community celebrates the (Fourth of July/fourth of July) with entertainment and fireworks.

955. I wasn't (ever/never) told to take this highway to your house.

956. After giving the customer the change, (he/the clerk) heard the store's

closing bell.

957. The island is (inaccessible/accessible) except by boat.

958. I (have rung/have rang) her doorbell several times today.

959. Last year, Mark (chose/choose) our vacation week.

960. The employee (brought/bringed) a sick child to daycare.

961. The cleaning crew (had thrown/had threw) out my notes before I returned for them.

962. My thoroughly cleaned car (does/do) not stay clean for very long.

963. The farmer, along with his hired men, (harvests/harvest) the wheat.

964. This horse wins (more frequently/frequentlyer) than any other.

965. He lost his composure during the (worst/worse) battle of the war.

966. (Do/Does) the students understand it ?

967. We answer the (teacher's/teachers) questions every day.

968. Does John study (at/that) the library every day ?

969. Are we (going/go) to play baseball tomorrow ?

970. John is looking at (some/any) pictures.

971. George bought (a/an) toothbrush and (an/a) apple.

972. John (doesn't/don't) drink a large quantity of fruit juice in the morning.

973. This newspaper (doesn't/don't) give a great deal of news.

974. Three (people/person) write letters in this room in the morning.

975. Three hundred automobiles (leave/leaves) the factory in the morning.

976. The teacher (announced/announce) the examination to the students.

977. I didn't (choose/chose) the correct answer yesterday.

978. Mary (spent/spend) an hour in the library yesterday.

979. The thin student knows the answers. (He's/His) in my class.

980. The new teacher (read/readed) two interesting books in the library last night.

981. It is possible (that/what) George is going to study business administration.

982. It is very probable (that/how) you spend a lot of time in the laboratory.

983. You (must be able/must can) to run fast.

984. When we were in London we (were able to/could to) visit the British Museum.

985. Paul recently finished high school. Therefore, he (must be/can be) about eighteen years old.

986. Some of those sentences (might be/could be) difficult for the new students.

987. I can go, and John can too. I can go, and so (can John/John can).

988. Mary can't go, and Helen can't either. Mary can't go, and neither (can Helen/Helen can).

989. We can improve our pronunciation by (imitating/imitate) native speakers.

990. We learn the meaning of new words by (looking/to look) them up in a dictionary.

991. The windows are clear. We (can/can not) look through them.

992. Diamonds are valuable. You (shouldn't/should) throw them away.

993. The meeting is very important. John (shouldn't/should) miss it.

994. It's an hour and (a half/half) by plane from Maryland to New York.

995. There weren't (any/some) pieces of bread on the table yesterday.

996. There's going to be (some/any) homework for us to do tomorrow.

997. Everyone knows how (well/good) he can speak English now.

998. What are you going to do when you (leave/left) the United States ?

999. Does he (want/wants) a course in English or a course in geography ?

第十六章 | # 標準答案（Answer keys）

1. rose 動詞過去式
2. known 動詞片語過去完成式
3. laid 動詞片語現在完成式
4. worn 動詞片語過去完成式
5. shrunk 動詞片語過去完成式
6. badly 副詞
7. loudly 副詞
8. well 副詞
9. quickly 副詞
10. ready 形容詞
11. politely 副詞
12. immaturely 副詞
13. immediately 副詞
14. well 副詞
15. quickly 副詞
16. lazily 副詞
17. quick 形容詞
18. sincerely 副詞
19. deeply 副詞
20. loud 形容詞
21. carefully 副詞
22. well 副詞
23. gives 動詞單數

24. give 動詞複數

25. gives 動詞單數

26. is 動詞單數

27. Whom 代名詞受格

28. Who 代名詞主格

29. whom 代名詞受格

30. Who 代名詞主格

31. Whom 代名詞受格

32. he 代名詞主格

33. I 代名詞主格

34. We 代名詞主格

35. They 代名詞主格

36. She/he 代名詞主格

37. Who 代名詞主格

38. she 代名詞主格

39. Who 代名詞主格

40. I 代名詞主格

41. his 代名詞所有格

42. my 代名詞所有格

43. their 代名詞所有格

44. your 代名詞所有格

45. whose 代名詞所有格

46. whom 代名詞受格

47. them 代名詞受格

48. them 代名詞受格

49. him 代名詞受格

50. her 代名詞受格

51. himself 反身代名詞單數

52. their 代名詞所有格

53. his 代名詞所有格單數

54. their 代名詞所有格複數

55. July 月份要大寫

56. raised 易混淆版字

57. Los Angeles, California 地名要大寫

58. tried 易混淆的字

59. Latin 專有名詞要大寫

60. checkers. Kelly 標點符號句號

61. game.標點符號句號

62. two 易混淆的字

63. in 介詞

64. uses 易混淆的字

65. umbrella.標點符號句號

66. store ?標點符號疑問號

67. attic.標點符號句號

68. district.標點符號句號

69. grandmother.標點符號句號

70. am !標點符號驚嘆號

71. mailbox.標點符號句號

71. is !標點符號驚嘆號

72. hamburgers ?標點符號疑問號

74. lesson ?標點符號疑問號

75. need 動詞複數

76. is 動詞單數

77. have 動詞複數

78. doesn't 助動詞單數

79. Were 動詞複數

80. play 動詞複數

81. were 動詞複數

82. Were 動詞複數

83. don't 助動詞複數

84. come 動詞複數

85. is 動詞單數

86. are 動詞複數

87. have 動詞複數

88. consider 動詞複數

89. creates 動詞單數

90. are 動詞複數

91. call 動詞複數

92. cans 動詞單數

93. catch 動詞複數

94. have 動詞片語複數現在完成式

95. have 動詞複數

96. were 動詞複數

97. were 動詞複數

98. go 動詞複數

99. have 動詞片語複數現在完成式

100. are 動詞複數

101. are 動詞複數

102. raid 動詞複數

103. were 動詞複數

104. go 動詞複數

105. bloom 動詞複數

106. belong 動詞複數

107. are 動詞複數

108. lies 動詞單數

109. is 動詞單數

110. teaches 動詞單數

111. are 動詞複數

112. are 動詞複數

113. deliver 動詞複數

114. have 動詞片語複數現在完成式

115. sweeps 動詞單數

116. have 動詞片語複數現在完成式

117. have 動詞片語複數現在完成式

118. makes 動詞單數

119. are 動詞複數

120. were 動詞複數

121. depends 動詞單數

122. need 動詞複數

123. are 動詞複數

124. are 動詞複數

125. Have 動詞片語複數現在完成式

126. Have 動詞片語複數現在完成式

127. Have 動詞片語複數現在完成式

128. There's 單數動詞即 is

129. are 動詞複數

130. Were 動詞複數

131. is 動詞單數

132. There are 動詞複數

133. Here are 動詞複數

134. was 動詞單數

135. sit 動詞複數

136. appeal 動詞複數

137. Were 動詞複數

138. doesn't 助動詞單數

139. are 動詞複數

140. Here are 動詞複數

141. are 動詞複數

142. don't 助動詞複數

143. look 動詞複數

144. has 動詞單數

145. go 動詞複數

146. weren't 動詞第二人稱

147. are 動詞複數

148. are 動詞複數

149. have 動詞片語複數現在完成式

150. are 動詞複數

151. am 動詞片語現在進行式

152. doesn't 助動詞單數

153. don't 助動詞複數

154. drunk 動詞片語現在完成式

155. known 動詞片語過去完成式

156. swam 動詞過去式

157. did 動詞過去式

158. frozen 動詞片語現在完成式

159. stolen 動詞片語現在完成式

160. broken 動詞片語現在完成式

161. given 動詞片語現在完成式

162. sung 動詞片語現在完成式

163. blown 動詞片語現在完成式

164. rang 動詞過去式

165. sank 動詞過去式

166. came 動詞過去式

167. saw 動詞過去式

168. thrown 動詞片語現在完成式

169. burst 動詞片語現在完成式

170. ridden 動詞片語現在完成式

171. worn 動詞片語過去完成式

172. begun 動詞片語過去完成式

173. fallen 動詞片語現在完成式

174. swum 動詞片語過去完成式

175. driven 動詞片語現在完成式

176. run 動詞片語現在完成式

177. shrank 動詞過去式

178. brought 動詞片語現在完成式

179. gone 動詞片語現在完成式

180. written 動詞片語現在完成式

181. chosen 動詞片語現在完成式

182. ran 動詞過去式

183. spoken 動詞片語現在完成式

184. sat 動詞片語過去完成式

185. set 易混淆的字

186. laid 易混淆的字

187. lain 易混淆的字

188. raised 易混淆的字

189. lay 易混淆的字

190. sits 易混淆的字

191. rising 易混淆的字

192. raises 易混淆的字

193. lying 易混淆的字

194. He 代名詞主格

195. she 代名詞主格

196. He 代名詞主格

197. I 代名詞主格

198. he 代名詞主格
199. We 代名詞主格
200. he 代名詞主格
201. they 代名詞主格
202. she 代名詞主格
203. she 代名詞主格
204. he 代名詞主格
205. I 代名詞主格
206. we 代名詞主格
207. they 代名詞主格
208. we 代名詞主格
209. he 代名詞主格
210. I 代名詞主格
211. he/she 均為代名詞主格
212. I 代名詞主格
213. we 代名詞主格
214. we 代名詞主格
215. he 代名詞主格
216. they 代名詞主格
217. she/they 均為代名詞主格
218. they 代名詞主格
219. I 代名詞主格
220. us 代名詞受格
221. them 代名詞受格
222. her/me 均為代名詞受格
223. me 代名詞受格
224. us 代名詞受格
225. us 代名詞受格
226. him 代名詞受格

227. me 代名詞受格
228. her/me 均為代名詞受格
229. us/them 均為代名詞受格
230. us/them 均為代名詞受格
231. him/her 均為代名詞受格
232. him 代名詞受格
233. him 代名詞受格
234. us 代名詞受格
235. her 代名詞受格
236. good 形容詞
237. taller 形容詞比較級
238. well 副詞
239. more clearly 副詞比較級
240. most slowly 副詞最高級
241. darkest 形容詞最高級
242. more attentive 形容詞比較級
243. most amazing 形容詞最高級
244. fiercely 副詞
245. heaviest 形容詞最高級
246. saddest 形容詞最高級
247. warmer 形容詞比較級
248. good 形容詞
249. better 形容詞比較級
250. funniest 形容詞最高級
251. anything 一次否定
252. anyone 一次否定
253. anything 一次否定
254. never 一次否定
255. worse 形容詞比較級

256. spring 四季不需大寫

257. Prize 專有名詞大寫

258. June 月份要大寫

259. art 非專有名詞不需大寫

260. Mount 專有名詞大寫

261. Africa 地名大寫

262. Mother's 特殊日子大寫

263. Memorial 專有名詞大寫

264. Senate/House/Representatives 專有名詞大寫

265. Fourth 國慶日大寫

266. Monument 專有名詞大寫

267. Highway 公路名詞大寫

268. October 月份大寫

269. Judge 職稱與名字連用要大寫

270. Senator Smith 職稱與名字連用要大寫

271. River 河流名要大寫

272. War 二戰要大寫

273. P.M.指下午要大寫

274. !驚嘆號

275. sunny and 只有兩個不需要點號

276. ancient bicycle 兩者密切無點號

277. stately pine 兩者密切無點號

278. jour-ney 以音節分開

279. rye bread 單音節不可分開

280. across 單音節不可分開

281. courses 易混淆的字

282. desert 易混淆的字

283. week 易混淆的字

284. two, stationery 易混淆的字

285. principal/hear 易混淆的字

286. Tom, who 要加點號

287. show, which 要加點號

288. record, which 要加點號

289. coin, which 要加點號

290. coin that 不需要點號

291. her 代名詞所有格

292. my 代名詞所有格

293. their 代名詞所有格

294. completely 副詞

295. violently 副詞

296. accurately 副詞

297. According to 副詞片語

298. into 易混淆的字

299. except 易混淆的字

300. and 連接詞

301. neither 連接詞成對

302. but also 連接詞成對

303. for 連接詞

304. nor 連接詞一致性

305. but 連接詞符合文義

306. for 連接詞符合文義

307. volunteering 動名詞

308. Shouting 現在分詞

309. warning 現在分詞

310. their 代名詞所有格

311. darting 動名詞

312. to move 不定詞

313. to teach 不定詞

314. to become 不定詞

315. who died 代名詞主格

316. when 連接詞符合文義

317. Since medicine 需要連接詞

318. which 連接詞

319. who 代名詞主格

320. whose 代名詞所有格

321. whose 代名詞所有格

322. to whom 介詞受詞受格

323. After 連接詞

324. Whoever 代名詞主格

325. what 代名詞

326. what 代名詞

327. That 連接詞

328. after 連接詞

329. in which 代名詞

330. until 連接詞

331. who 代名詞主格

332. nor 連接詞符合文義

333. but 連接詞

334. will take 動詞片語未來式

335. before 連接詞

336. After 連接詞

337. needs 動詞單數

338. is 動詞單位

339. are 動詞複數

340. have 動詞片語複數現在完成式

341. has 動詞片語單數現在完成式

342. their 代名詞所有格

343. their 代名詞所有格

344. its 代名詞單數所有格

345. them 代名詞複數受格

346. them 代名詞複數受格

347. their 代名詞複數所有格

348 their 代名詞複數所有格

349. attracts 動詞單數

350. is 動詞單數

351. need 動詞複數

352. is 動詞單數

353. play 動詞複數

354. grow 動詞複數

355. have 動詞片語複數現在完成式

356. taste 動詞複數

357. likes 動詞單數

358. take 動詞複數

359. displays 動詞單數

360. harmonize 動詞複數

361. wants 動詞單數

362. wonder 動詞複數

363. were 動詞複數

364. are 動詞複數

365. are 動詞複數

366. bear 動詞複數

367. calls 動詞單數

368. mow 動詞複數

369. bloom 動詞複數

370. digs 動詞單數

371. crack 動詞複數

372. provides 動詞單數

373. have 動詞片語複數現在完成被動式

374. realize 動詞複數

375. were 動詞片語多數過去進行式

376. are 動詞複數現在進行式

377. Here are 動詞複數

378. differ 動詞複數

379. There are 動詞複數

380. Where are 動詞複數

381. doesn't 助動詞單數

382. don't 助動詞複數

383. Doesn't 助動詞單數

384. costs 動詞單數

385. leave 動詞複數

386. Don't 助動詞第二人稱

387. disappears 動詞單數

388. agree 動詞複數

389. she 代名詞主格

390. his 代名詞所有格

391. his 代名詞所有格單數

392. her 代名詞所有格單數

393. their 代名詞所有格複數

394. we 代名詞主格複數

395. their 代名詞所有格複數

396. their 代名詞所有格複數

397. their 代名詞所有格複數

398. their 代名詞所有格複數

399. her 代名詞所有格單數

400. its 代名詞所有格單數

401. his 代名詞所有格單數

402. goes 動詞單數

403. has 動詞片語單數現在完成式

404. take 動詞複數

405. has 動詞單數現在完成式

406. his 代名詞所有格單數

407. to bed 不定詞

408. its 代名詞所有格單數

409. its 代名詞所有格單數

410. their 代名詞所有格複數

411. itself 反身代名詞單數

412. their 代名詞所有格複數

413. them 代名詞受格複數

414. chose 動詞過去式

415. asked 動詞過去式

416. rang 動詞過去式

417. froze 動詞過去式

418. shrank 動詞過去式

419. sat 動詞過去式

420. drank 動詞過去式

421. set 易混淆的字

422. setting 易混淆的字

423. lie 易混淆的字

424. lain 易混淆的字

425. rising 易混淆的字

426. raise 易混淆的字

427. risen 易混淆的字

428. lies 易混淆的字

429. set/lay 均為易混淆的字

430. rise 易混淆的字

431. lying 易混淆的字

432. ridden/brought 動詞片語過去完成式和假設語氣

433. frozen 動詞片語假設語氣

434. found 動詞過去式

435. him 代名詞受格

436. them 代名詞受格

437. they 代名詞主格

438. we 代名詞主格

439. he 代名詞主格

440. she 代名詞主格

441. us 代名詞受格

442. us 代名詞受格

443. they 代名詞主格

444. I 代名詞主格

445. them 代名詞受格

446. us 代名詞受格

447. him 代名詞受格

448. me 代名詞受格

449. me 代名詞受格

450. her 代名詞受格

451. me 代名詞受格

452. couldn't 一次否定

453. most 副詞最高級

454. more 副詞比較級

455. easier 形容詞比較級

456. any other city 主體要排除在外

457. anyone else 主體要排除在外

458. War 越戰要大寫

459. Revolution 美國革命戰爭要大寫

460. South American 特指美國南方要大寫

461. Brazil/Portuguese 國家語言要大寫

462. is ?問句要疑問號

463. falling,標點符號要點號

464. tonight,標點符號要點號

465. Jupiter,/sun,兩個都要點號

466. advises 易混淆的字

467. all right 易混淆的字

468. then 易混淆的字

469. then 易混淆的字

470. synthetic 易混淆的字

471. annals 易混淆的字

472. humiliating 易混淆的字

473. guile 易混淆的字

474. hypothesis 易混淆的字

475. fed 易混淆的字

476. invincible 易混淆的字

477. in 介詞

478. of/of 均為介詞

479. for 介詞

480. of/with 均為介詞

481. with/without 均為介詞

482. or 連接詞成對

483. yet 連接詞否定用

484. have 動詞片語現在完成式

485. chases 動詞單數

486. secludes 動詞單數

487. questions 名詞多數

488. are 動詞多數

489. are 動詞多數

490. won 動詞過去式

491. stood 動詞過去式

492. prancing 現在分詞

493. Swaggering 現在分詞

494. Leaving 現在分詞

495. banging 現在分詞

496. Terrified 過去分詞

497. Walking 動名詞

498. passing 動名詞

499. woodworking 動名詞

500. giving 現在分詞

501. To dance 不定詞

502. to lose/to eat 均為不定詞

503. to get/to take 均為不定詞

504. to review 不定詞

505. Sold 過去分詞

506. published 動詞片語被動式

507. video that 不需要標點符號

508. Griffins, which 需要點號

509. data on 不需要標點符號

510. wants 動詞單數

511. are 動詞複數

512. want 動詞複數

513. is 動詞單數

514. tells 動詞單數

515. show 動詞複數

516. is 動詞單數

517. have 動詞複數

518. continue 動詞複數

519. solves 動詞單數

520. contains 動詞單數

521. does not 助動詞單數

522. makes 動詞單數

523. thrown 動詞片語現在完成式

524. blew 動詞過去式

525. her 代名詞受格

526. her 代名詞受格

527. me 代名詞受格

528. me/we 代名詞受格和主格

529. She 代名詞主格

530. she/us 代名詞主格和受格

531. me 代名詞受格

532. her 代名詞受格

533. he/I 均為代名詞主格

534. they 代名詞主格

535. me 代名詞受格

536. to whom 介詞接代名詞受格

537. who 代名詞主格

538. whom 介詞接代名詞受格

539. who 代名詞主格

540. whom 代名詞受格

541. they/we 均為代名詞主格

542. I 代名詞主格

543. He 代名詞主格

544. most 形容詞最高級

545. affected 易混淆的字

546. Besides 易混淆的字

547. etc. 易混淆的字

548. take 易混淆的字

549. as fast as 易混淆的字

550. Everywhere 易混淆的字

551. accepted 易混淆的字

552. have 動詞片語假設語氣

553. ought not 易混淆的字

554. taught 易混淆的字

555. Unless 連接詞

556. those/that 代名詞複數和單數

557. that/anywhere 代名詞和易混淆的字

558. Those 代名詞複數

559. who 代名詞指人

560. unless 連接詞

561. have 動詞片語現在完成式肯定意味

562. any 一次否定

563. ever/anyone 一次否定

564. Methodist 專有名詞要大寫

565. Chemistry/Latin 均為專有名詞要大寫

566. Hurricane/Allen 均為專有名詞要大寫

567. Olympics/Los Angeles 均為專有名詞要大寫

568. , by the way, 要兩個點號

569. cool, dark 要點號

570. paper plates,要點號

571. Well,/Ted !要點號和驚嘆號

572. batter, hoping/,laid 均要點號

573. , one kind of living organism,要兩個點號

574. , a member of the audience, 要兩個點號

575. Consequently,要點號

576. bluebonnet,/lupine ?要點號和疑問號

577. Theirs 易混淆的字

578. their 易混淆的字

579. whose 易混淆的字

580. one's 易混淆的字

581. one-half/thirty-five 兩個均要連字號

582. peace 易混淆的字

583. formally 易混淆的字

584. whether 易混淆的字

585. waste 易混淆的字

586. to go, I'll go with you.要完整的句子

587. She was elected 要完整的句子

588. heat, they/mountains, setting 均要點號

589. known 動詞片語被動式

590. sends 動詞單數

591. who 代名詞

592. that 連接詞

593. who 代名詞

594. so that 連接詞

595. as though 連接詞

596. has 動詞片語現在完成進行式

597. are 動詞複數

598. were 動詞複數過去被動式

599. is 動詞單數

600. is 動詞單數現在進行式

601. are 動詞複數

602. meet 動詞複數

603. has 動詞片語現在完成式

604. gives 動詞單數

605. counts 動詞單數

606. is 動詞單數

607. comes 動詞單數

608. is 動詞單數

609. are 動詞複數

610. their 代名詞所有格複數

611. their 代名詞所有格複數

612. their 代名詞所有格複數

613. its 代名詞所有格單數

614. is 動詞單數

615. was 動詞單數

616. he 代名詞單數

617. is 動詞單數

618. were 動詞複數

619. is 動詞單數

620. he 代名詞單數

621. his 代名詞所有格單數

622. its 代名詞所有格單數

623. is 動詞單數

624. she 代名詞主格

625. whoever 代名詞主格

626. who 代名詞主格

627. I 代名詞主格

628. who 代名詞主格

629. she 代名詞主格

630. she/I 代名詞均為主格

631. us/we 代名詞受格和主格

632. her/me 代名詞均為受格

633. whom 代名詞受格

634. me 代名詞受格

635. him/me 代名詞均為受格

636. whom 代名詞受格

637. him 代名詞受格

638. lain 易混淆的字

639. lying 易混淆的字

640. rising 易混淆的字

641. worst 形容詞最高級

642. bad 形容詞

643. more useful 形容詞比較級

644. sweeter 形容詞比較級

645. Since 連接詞

646. illusion 易混淆的字

647. fewer 形容詞可數比較級

648. have 易混淆的字

649. rather 易混淆的字

650. occurs 易混淆的字

651. means that 易混淆的字

652. who 連接詞指人

653. that 連接詞

654. doesn't/that 助動詞單數和代名詞

655. emigrated 易混淆的字

656. this 形容詞

657. space shuttle 非特定不要大寫

658. Gloria,要點號

659. carrier, does 要點號

660. the rings, and 要點號

661. time; however 要分號

662. dog; it 要分號

663. contest; therefore 要分號

664. follows; remove 要分號

665. who's/their 均為易混淆的字

666. you're/it's 均為易混淆的字

667. waist 易混淆的字

668. Whether 易混淆的字

669. has borrowed 動詞片語單數現在完成式

670. sounds 動詞單數

671. remain 動詞複數

672. was 動詞單數

673. could detect 動詞片語

674. had been 動詞片語過去完成被動式

675. haven't seen 動詞片語現在完成式

676. Having 現在分詞片語被動式

677. it bursting 現在分詞

678. to sell 不定詞

679. people 名詞多數

680. offers 動詞單數

681. results 動詞單數

682. work 動詞複數

683. her 代名詞單數

684. attracts 動詞單數

685. are 動詞複數

686. is 動詞單數

687. advocate 動詞複數

688. has 動詞片語現在完成被動式單數

689. makes 動詞單數

690. has 動詞片語單數現在完成式

691. is 動詞單數

692. is 動詞單數

693. is 動詞單數

694. Does 助動詞單數

695. is 動詞單數

696. don't 助動詞複數

697. were 動詞複數被動式

698. are 動詞複數

699. is 動詞單數

700. is 動詞單數

701. enroll 動詞多數

702. themselves 反身代名詞複數

703. are 動詞複數

704. have 動詞複數

705. give 動詞複數

706. plans 動詞單數

707. are 動詞單數

708. makes 動詞單數

709. me 代名詞受格

710. he 代名詞主格

711. I 代名詞主格

712. She and I 代名詞主格

713. Whom 代名詞受格

714. her 代名詞受格

715. them 代名詞受格

716. me 代名詞受格

717. she 代名詞主格

718. we 代名詞主格

719. whom 代名詞受格

720. me 代名詞受格

721. We 代名詞主格

722. she/whom 代名詞主格和受格

723. whoever 代名詞主格

724. whom 代名詞受格

725. us 代名詞受格

726. to go 不定詞現在式

727. were 動詞假設語氣

728. have missed 動詞片語現在完成式

729. had left 動詞片語過去完成式

730. burst 易混淆的字

731. must have broken 動詞片語假設語氣

732. rung 動詞片語現在完成式

733. torn 動詞片語被動式

734. stolen 動詞片語被動式

735. blown 動詞片語被動式

736. chosen 動詞片語過去完成式

737. Lie 易混淆的字

738. lies 易混淆的字

739. lay 易混淆的字

740. sat 易混淆的字

741. sit 易混淆的字

742. rising 易混淆的字

743. lain 易混淆的字

744. lying 易混淆的字

745. laid 易混淆的字

746. have taken 動詞片語現在完成式

747. bit 動詞過去式

748. will have stopped 動詞片語未來完成式

749. will have been married 動詞片語未來完成被動式

750. had asked 動詞片語假設語氣

751. were cataloged 動詞片語假設語氣

752. are 動詞複數

753. were created 動詞片語被動式

754. had listened 動詞片語假設語氣

755. had been waiting 動詞片語過去完成進行式

756. had revised 動詞片語假設語氣

757. to protect 不定詞現在式

758. will have heard 動詞片語未來完成式

759. have lain 動詞片語現在完成式

760. had remembered 動詞片語假設語氣

761. lay 易混淆的字

762. had offered 動詞片語假設語氣

763. smelled 動詞過去式

764. am 動詞現在式

765. were 動詞過去式

766. had seen 動詞片語假設語氣

767. concluded 動詞過去式

768. will have learned 動詞片語未來完成式

769. to survive 不定詞現在式

770. had taken 動詞片語假設語氣

771. were 動詞片語假設語氣

772. is lying 易混淆的字

773. wonderful 形容詞最高級

774. any other 比較時主體要排除

775. cautiously 副詞

776. steadily 副詞

777. less 副詞比較級

778. anyone else's 比較時本體要排除

779. well 副詞

780. strangely 副詞

781. continually 副詞

782. clearly 副詞

783. skeptically 副詞

784. badly 副詞

785. bad 形容詞

786. well 副詞

787. quickly 副詞

788. than anyone else 比較時本體要排除

789. best match 形容詞比較最高級

790. hardest 形容詞比較最高級

791. seriously 副詞

792. well 副詞

793. worse 形容詞比較級

794. bigger 形容詞比較級

795. more seriously 副詞比較級

796. feeling 現在分詞

797. could/have 一次否定和易混淆的字

798. as it 連接詞

799. Can't any 一次否定

800. kind of 易混淆的字

801. number 易混淆的字

802. everywhere 易混淆的字

803. take 易混淆的字

804. as far as 易混淆的字

805. among 易混淆的字

806. did 動詞過去式

807. like 介詞

808. that 連接詞

809. somewhat 副詞

810. any 一次否定

811. anything 一次否定

812. could barely 一次否定

813. can't help feeling 現在分詞

814. Besides 易混淆的字

815. fewer 易混淆的字

816. immediately ! 標點符號驚嘆號

817. its 易混淆的字

818. whose 易混淆的字

819. clothes 易混淆的字

820. compliments 易混淆的字

821. dessert/desert 易混淆的字

822. latter 易混淆的字

823. principal 易混淆的字

824. loose 易混淆的字

825. your/whose/theirs 均為易混淆的字

826. argument, I 需要點號

827. mail, she 需要點號

828. themselves 反身代名詞複數

829. our 代名詞所有格

830. or 連接詞成對

831. and 連接詞成對

832. someone who 不需要標點符號

833. report, is 需要點號

834. one that 不需要標點符號

835. forecaster whom 代名詞受格

836. and I 需要連接詞

837. in fact,連接詞

838. what 連接詞

839. Although this 連接詞

840. would 助動詞過去式

841. There 易混淆的字

842. has 動詞單數

843. Is 動詞單數

844. has 動詞單數

845. is 動詞單數

846. was 動詞單數

847. her 代名詞所有格單數

848. has 動詞片語單數現在完成式

849. forces 動詞單數

850. is 動詞單數

851. are 動詞複數

852. sounds 動詞單數

853. is 動詞單數

854. have disagreed 動詞片語多數現在完成式

855. comes 動詞單數

856. is 動詞單數

857. comes 動詞單數

858. is 動詞單數

859. has 動詞單數

860. was 動詞單數

861. finishes 動詞單數

862. represent 動詞複數

863. is 動詞單數

864. offend 動詞複數

865. happen 動詞複數

866. its 代名詞所有格單數

867. her 代名詞所有格單數

868. have 動詞複數

869. stays 動詞單數

870. were 動詞複數

871. retires 動詞單數

872. will have 動詞片語未來式

873. Are 動詞複數

874. was 動詞單數

875. needs 動詞單數

876. their 代名詞所有格複數

877. my 代名詞所有格

878. us 代名詞受格

879. whom 代名詞受格

880. her 代名詞受格

881. me 代名詞受格

882. she 代名詞主格

883. us 代名詞受格

884. him 代名詞受格

885. whom 代名詞受格

886. who 代名詞主格

887. who 代名詞主格

888. whom 代名詞受格

889. who 代名詞主格

890. my making 代名詞所有格

891. she 代名詞主格

892. her 代名詞所有格

893. whom 代名詞受格

894. us 代名詞受格
895. had 動詞片語假設語氣
896. to have qualified 不定詞完成式
897. were 動詞假設語氣
898. were drawn 動詞片語被動語態
899. has driven 動詞片語現在完成式
900. sang 動詞過去式
901. had called 動詞片語假設語氣
902. had forgotten 動詞片語假設語氣
903. had lost 動詞片語假設語氣
904. to avoid 不定詞現在式
905. had done 動詞片語過去完成式
906. had taken 動詞片語過去完成式
907. had had 動詞片語假設語氣
908. had checked 動詞片語假設語氣
909. are 動詞現在式
910. had had 動詞片語假設語氣
911. sharply 副詞
912. bad 形容詞
913. slowly 副詞
914. nervous 形容詞
915. clearer 形容詞比較級
916. the lesser 形容詞比較級
917. good 形容詞
918. better 副詞比較級
919. gradually 副詞
920. is only 動詞不可省略
921. likely 易混淆的字
922. that 連接詞

923. something 一次否定

924. nauseated 易混淆的字

925. that 連接詞

926. Naturally, 需要點號

927. up 副詞

928. through 介詞

929. among 介詞

930. into 介詞

931. after 介詞

932. have figured 動詞片語現在完成式

933. has become 動詞片語現在完成式

934. whom 代名詞受格

935. Who 代名詞主格

936. me 代名詞受格

937. your 代名詞所有格

938. she 代名詞主格

939. she 代名詞主格

940. consumer 對象要一致性

941. Unless 連接詞

942. but also 連接詞成對

943. and they 需要連接詞

944. and play 需要連接詞

945. the child 對象要一致性

946. wheel because 受詞和連接詞

947. where 連接詞

948. it was 主詞不可省略

949. came after 動詞過去式

950. had cooked 動詞片語過去完成式

951. why, it 需要點號

952. ex-Senator 需要連字號

953. history 普通名詞小寫

954. Fourth of July 專有名詞要大寫

955. ever 一次否定

956. he 主詞一致性

957. inaccessible 易混淆的字

958. have rung 動詞片語現在完成式

959. chose 動詞過去式

960. brought 動詞過去式

961. had thrown 動詞片語過去完成式

962. does 助動詞單數

963. harvests 動詞單數

964. more frequently 副詞比較級

965. worst 形容詞最高級

966. Do 助動詞複數

967. teacher's 易混淆的字

968. at 介詞

969. going 動詞片語現在進行式

970. some 形容詞肯定意味

971. a/an 均為易混淆的字

972. doesn't 助動詞單數

973. doesn't 助動詞單數

974. people 名詞複數

975. leave 動詞複數

976. announced 動詞過去式

977. choose 動詞原型

978. spent 動詞過去式

979. He's 易混淆的字

980. read 動詞過去式

981. that 連接詞

982. that 連接詞

983. must be able 動詞片語假設語氣

984. were able to 動詞片語過去式

985. must be 動詞片語假設語氣

986. might be 動詞片語假設語氣

987. can John 倒裝句

988. can Helen 倒裝句

989. imitating 動名詞

990. looking 動名詞

991. can 助動詞肯定意味

992. shouldn't 助動詞否定意味

993. shouldn't 助動詞否定意味

994. a half 要有冠詞

995. any 形容詞否定

996. some 形容詞肯定

997. well 副詞

998. leave 動詞現在式

999. want 動詞原型

第十七章 ｜ 文法用語中英文對照表

（Grammatical Terms Chinese English Table）

1. 冠詞——Article
   不定冠詞（indefinite article）
   限定冠詞（definite article）
   母音（vowel）
   子音（consonnant sound）
2. 副詞——Adverb
   簡單副詞（或稱單字副詞）（simple adverb）
   疑問副詞（interrogative adverb）
   關係副詞（relative adverb）
   情狀副詞（adverb of manner）
   時間副詞（adverb of time）
   頻率副詞（adverb of frequency）
   地方副詞（adverb of place）
   程度副詞（adverb of degree）
   肯定或否定副詞（adverb of affirmation and negation）
   副詞的形成（formation of adverb）
   副詞的比較（comparison of adverb）
   原級（positive degree）
   比較級（comparative degree）
   最高級（superlative degree）
   修飾（modify）

3. 介詞——Preposition

簡單介詞（simple preposition）

雙重介詞（double preposition）

片語介詞（phrase preposition）

4. 名詞——Noun

主詞（subject）

受詞（object）

直接受詞（direct object）

間接受詞（indirect object）

可數名詞（countable noun）

不可數名詞（uncountable noun）

普通名詞（common noun）

集合名詞（collective noun）

專有名詞（proper noun）

物質名詞（material noun）

抽象名詞（abstract noun）

複合名詞（compound noun）

同位語（apposition）

動名詞（gerund）

名詞的數（number of noun）

單數（singular）

複數（plural）

名詞的性（genders of noun）

雄性（masculine gender）

雌性（feminine gender）

中性（common gender）

無性（neuter gender）

名詞的格（cases of noun）

主格（nominative case）

受格（objective case）

所有格（possessive case）

主格補語（subjective complement）

受格補語（objective complement）

5. 代名詞——Pronoun

人稱代名詞（personal pronoun）

反身代名詞（亦稱複合人身代詞, compound personal pronoun）

指示代名詞（demonstrative pronoun）

關係代名詞（relative pronoun）

疑問代名詞（interrogative pronoun）

不定代名詞（indefinite pronoun）

第一人稱（first person）

第二人稱（second person）

第三人稱（third person）

限定用法（restrictive use）

非限定用法（non restrictive use）

雙重所有（double possive）

所有代名詞（possessive pronoun）

先行詞（antecedent）

6. 形容詞——adjective

普通形容詞（又稱敘述形容詞）（descriptive adjective）

專有形容詞（proper adjective）

代名形容詞（pronominal adjective）

數量形容詞（quantitative adjective）

複合形容詞（compound adjective）

形容詞相等語（adjective equivalent）

物質形容詞（material adjective）

數字形容詞（numberal adjective）

基數（cardinal）

序數（ordinal）

倍數（multiplicative）

形容詞的比較（comparison of adjective）

原級（positive degree）

比較級（comparative degree）

最高級（superlative degree）

補語形容詞（predicate adjective）

形容詞的形成（form of adjective）

7. 連接詞——conjunction

簡單連接詞（simple conjunction）

對等連接詞（co-ordinate conjunction）

相關連接詞（correlative conjunction）

從屬連接詞（subordinate conjunction）

相關從屬連接詞（corretative subordinate conjunction）

片語連接詞（phrase conjunction）

副詞連接詞（adverbial conjunction）

8. 感嘆詞——Interjection

情緒（emotion）

感受（feeling）

興奮（excitement）

9. 動詞——Verb

動作動詞（action verb）

看得見的動作（visible action）

心裡的活動（mental action）

及物動詞（transitive verb）

不完全及物動詞（incomplete transitive verb）

不及物動詞（intransitive verb）

不完成不及物動詞（incomplete intransitive verb）

連繫動詞（linking verb）

情緒動詞（emotive verb）

限定動詞（finite verb）

非限定動詞（non-finite verb）

規則動詞（regular verb）

不規則動詞（irregular verb）

主動詞（main verb）

助動詞（auxiliary or helping verb）

不定詞（infinitive）

動詞的三主要部分（the three principal parts of verbs）

原型動詞（root form）

現在式（present form）

過去式（past form）

現在分詞（present participle）

過去分詞（past participle）

動詞時態（verb tense）

簡單現在式（simple present）

簡單過去式（simple past）

簡單未來式（simple future）

現在完成式（present perfect）

過去完成式（past perfect）

未來完成式（future perfect）

簡單現在進行式（simple present progressive）

簡單過去進行式（simple past progressive）

簡單未來進行式（simple future progressive）

現在完成進行式（present perfect progressive）

過去完成進行式（past perfect progressive）

未來完成進行式（future perfect progressive）

動詞語氣（verb mood）

陳述語氣（indicative mood）

假設語氣（subjunctive mood）

祈使語氣（imperative mood）

動詞語態（verb voice）

主動語態（active voice）

被動語態（passive voice）

動作的執行者（performer of action）

動作的接受者（receiver of action）

現在非事實（present-unreal）

過去非事實（past-unreal）

未來非事實（future-unreal）

未來有可能（future-possible）

未來不確定（future uncertain）

現在簡單被動式（present simple passive voice）

過去簡單被動式（past simple passive voice）

未來簡單被動式（future simple passive voice）

現在進行被動式（present progressive passive voice）

過去進行被動式（past progressive passive voice）

現在完成被動式（present perfect progressive passive voice）

過去完成被動式（past perfect progressive passive voice）

未來完成被動式（future perfect progressive passive voice）

10. 片語——Phrase

形容詞片語（adjective phrase）

副詞片語（adverbial phrase）

名詞片語（noun phrase）

介詞片語（prepositional phrase）

現在分詞片語（present participle phrase）

過去分詞片語（past participle phrase）

動名詞片語（gerund phrase）

不定詞片語（infinitive phrase）

11. 子句──Clause　　句子──Sentence

　　獨立子句（亦稱主要子句）（independent clause or main clause）

　　附屬子句（亦稱從屬子句）（subordinate or dependent clause）

　　名詞子句（noun clause）

　　形容詞子句（adjective clause）

　　副詞子句（adverbial clause）

　　對等子句（coordinate clause）

　　主動（subject）

　　述動（predicate）

　　主詞（subject word）

　　述詞（predicate verb）

　　簡單句（simple sentence）

　　連合句（compound sentence）

　　複合句（complex sentence）

　　複連合句（compound-complex sentence）

　　敘述句（declarative sentence）

　　疑問句（interrogative sentence）

　　祈使句（imperative sentence）

　　感嘆句（exclamatory sentence）

　　連續的句子（run-on sentence）

　　連合主詞（compound subject）

　　平行構句（parallel structure）

　　直接敘述（direct narration）

　　間接敘述（indirect narration）

　　子句的減縮（clause reduce）

　　句子的減縮（sentence reduce）

　　避免冗長（avoid wordiness wordy）

　　避免重複（avoid repetition）

　　避免遺漏（avoid omission）

字的順序（word order）

倒裝句（inverted sentence）

12. 一致性——agreement

時態的一致（tense agreement）

肯定的一致（affirmative agreement）

否定的一致（negative agreement）

雙重否定（double negative）

13. 容易混淆的字——Common usage problem

14. 標點符號和簡寫——Punctuation & Contraction

劃底線（或斜體字）（underlining or italic）

雙引號（quotation）

單引號（single quotation mark）

句號（end mark）

疑問號（question mark）

點號（comma）

分號（semicolon）

冒號（colon）

縮減符號（abbreviation）

省略符號（contraction）

所有符號（apostrophe）

連字號（hyphen）

破折號（亦稱長劃符號）（dash）

括號（parenthesis）

括弧（bracket）

驚嘆號（exclamation point）

國家圖書館出版品預行編目資料

TOEFL 托福文法與構句　前冊／李英松著. —
初版.—新北市：李昭儀，2021.9
　　面；　公分
ISBN 978-957-43-8875-2（平裝）

1. 托福考試 2. 語法

805.1894　　　　　　　　　　　110007535

TOEFL托福文法與構句　前冊

作　　者　李英松
校　　對　李英松、李昭儀
發 行 人　李英松
出　　版　李昭儀
　　　　　E-mail：lambtyger@gmail.com
　　　　　郵政劃撥：李昭儀
　　　　　郵政劃撥帳號：0002566 0047109
設計編印　白象文化事業有限公司
　　　　　專案主編：水邊　　經紀人：洪怡欣
代理經銷　白象文化事業有限公司
　　　　　412台中市大里區科技路1號8樓之2（台中軟體園區）
　　　　　出版專線：（04）2496-5995　　傳真：（04）2496-9901
　　　　　401台中市東區和平街228巷44號（經銷部）
　　　　　購書專線：（04）2220-8589　　傳真：（04）2220-8505
印　　刷　普羅文化股份有限公司
初版一刷　2021 年 9 月
定　　價　400 元